RUMOR HAS IT

A DIRTY LOVE NOVELLA

R.L. KENDERSON

For Grayson

NOTE FROM THE AUTHOR

Dear Reader-

Rumor Has It was written after *Friends with Benefits*. *Friends with Benefits* was originally written as a standalone with no other books planned.

In *Friends with Benefits*, you meet Rachel & Sean who are engaged to be married. So, when we went back and wrote their story, we made their book the first in the series.

Because *Rumor Has It* was not planned at the time *Friends with Benefits* was written we ran into the problem of Rachel & Sean meeting in college but not getting married until a decade later.

Because of this, *Rumor Has It* is a little unconventional in that it spans about ten years. Their story starts as a resisting you romance and evolves into a second chance romance.

It is the only book in the series that takes place in college and can be considered new adult. It is also the only book that is a novella. The story is shorter than the other three in the series and is too quick for some readers. But we don't believe in adding fluff, aka making a book longer for the sake of making it longer.

If novella's aren't your thing, you may want to skip over it, and go straight to *Friends with Benefits*. Or come back and read *Rumor Has It* once you get a chance to meet Rachel & Sean. There is no right or wrong order to the read the books. The main thing is you enjoy them.

Thanks to all of you who read our books, and happy reading!

Renae & Lara
R.L. Kenderson

PROLOGUE

PRESENT DAY

Rachel Garwood—technically, it was Rachel King now—found a dark corner to sit, and she collapsed into the chair. She slipped off her high heels and put her feet up onto the chair next to her.

So far, her wedding day had been great, but she needed a break from being the center of attention and from dancing. Her wedding shoes were beautiful, but they hadn't been made for partying all night.

She pulled one of her feet onto her lap and inspected it. *Worth it.* After all, she was only getting married once.

She supposed everyone thought that, but for her, it was true. She knew that Sean was the only one for her.

She stretched her leg out and put her foot back with its partner as she looked out onto the dance floor. Her new husband was dancing with one of his brother's daughters standing on his feet. Behind the two of them was a line of several other nieces. Sean was going to be occupied for a while, giving Rachel the opportunity to relax.

She looked down at her new wedding ring and smiled. She couldn't believe she was finally married. She and Sean had years of history, and to think...if her alarm hadn't broken, the two of them might not be together.

CHAPTER ONE

TWELVE YEARS AGO

R achel, college freshman and queen of sleep, buried her nose in her pillow, not wanting to get out of bed yet.

It took her a few seconds to figure out what day it was— Tuesday. So, she had World Religions class first thing this morning. It was a good thing she'd woken up on her own because, apparently, Professor Drumming was one of the few teachers on campus who took attendance and counted absences and tardies against students' grades.

Rachel yawned and stretched her arms over her head. It felt good to get up without her alarm clock.

Wait a minute.

She never woke up on her own for class.

Rachel rolled over and looked at her alarm clock. The face was blank. In a panic, she reached for her phone. She flipped it open and shrieked so loudly, she woke her roommate.

"What? What?" Elise said as she sprang into a sitting position from her lofted bed and smacked her head on the ceiling. "*Ow!*" she said as she covered her injury with her hand.

"Elise, we have fifteen minutes to get to class," Rachel said as she jumped down from her loft and went searching for her toothbrush and clothes.

"What?" Elise said, her voice groggy and confused.

"We're going to be late. My stupid alarm clock broke."

"Crap," Elise said, jumping down next to Rachel.

"I'm sorry," Rachel told her roommate.

She hadn't met Elise until the day they moved into the dorms, but they'd clicked immediately and become instant friends. She'd won the roommate lotto for sure.

"For what? My head or your alarm?"

"Both."

"You're forgiven," Elise said with a smile. "We'd better hurry, huh?"

"Yes."

Both girls grabbed their toiletries and headed to the bathroom after getting dressed. They made do with the amount of time they had. That pretty much meant that they used the facilities, brushed their teeth, and combed their hair. There was no time for showers or makeup. That was fine with Rachel. She wasn't looking to impress anyone with her looks, just her grades.

An image of a guy in her class flashed across her brain, and she quickly dismissed it. She'd never even talked to him, and he was someone she wouldn't normally be attracted to. It was one of those weird body-chemistry things that she had no control over, and so far, she'd done a pretty good job of ignoring it.

Rachel and Elise ran out of their dorm and headed to class. Their classroom wasn't large, but it was seated stadium-style, so the doors were located at the back of the room. They headed for the first empty row they saw and moved in a few spots because neither of them liked sitting on the end.

Professor Drumming was facing the clock on the sidewall but turned to frown at their almost-tardy entrance before looking at the wall again. He did this at every class, and the minute class started, he would turn around and do roll call. Roll call. In college. Thank heavens it was the only class they had where a teacher did this.

Rachel followed the instructor's gaze to note that she and Elise had made it with about thirty seconds to spare. She'd known it would be close. As the clock neared the full hour, someone slipped into the seat next to her.

Rachel started to turn her head to look, but at the same time, Professor Drumming spun around and said, "Let's begin." He picked up his clipboard. "Jeff Anderson?"

"Here," a voice in the front of the room said.

Suddenly, the air around Rachel crackled, and a male voice spoke in her ear, "Doesn't he ever get tired of being a tight-ass?"

She slowly rotated her head, already knowing who the owner of the voice was due to the tingle going down her spine.

Sean King was sitting next to her, and Rachel felt her

breath catch. Even though he had arrived later to class than her, he smelled incredible and looked like he hadn't rolled out of bed like she had. His blond hair was styled, and his T-shirt and jeans looked like they hadn't been pulled from his bedroom floor. The light glinted off the silver ring he wore on his right middle finger, drawing her gaze to his narrow but masculine hands.

Thankfully, he was already facing the front of the room, so he couldn't see her reaction to him. He wasn't waiting for her response, and she doubted he felt the same way she did.

She didn't understand this unwanted attraction to Sean. He wasn't her type, and until this moment, they'd never spoken to each other. Sean was thin and on the shorter side, probably around five-seven or five-eight if she had to guess, and Rachel liked her men big and tall.

Hypocritical, she knew. At five-two and with the body of a twelve-year-old—aka small boobs and no butt—she shouldn't judge someone for being small or thin. But that was probably why she went for big men. She wanted her future offspring to have a chance at having some height.

Plus, she and her ex-boyfriend had dated for over a year and just broken up over the summer. Rachel wasn't really looking to start another relationship. She wanted to have some fun with being single in college for a while.

An elbow nudged her from the other side, rousing her from her thoughts.

"What?" she asked Elise, looking at her.

Her friend raised her brow and tilted her head toward the front of the room. "Your name was called."

A soft male chuckle sounded next to her.

"Here," Rachel called out and bent over toward her backpack, hiding her now-red face. She'd been so lost in thought, she hadn't heard the teacher. She "searched" for a pen for several seconds, willing her face to cool before she had to sit back up.

Elise leaned over next to her. "Are you okay?" she whispered.

Rachel hadn't told anyone about her weird attraction to Sean because she figured it was a biological fluke, assuming it would go away soon. She didn't want to make a big deal out of it by talking about it out loud.

"Yeah. Fine," she told her roommate and straightened. She smiled at Elise. "I think I'm half-asleep."

Elise grinned. "Me, too," she whispered. "We need to get coffee after this."

"Agreed."

Professor Drumming began his lecture, so Rachel was saved from having to look at Sean again or acknowledge his presence.

About twenty minutes into class, a woman came in the back door, approached the professor, and whispered in his ear.

Their instructor looked up at the class. "Please, excuse me. I have a phone call I need to take. Please look over your notes until I get back."

He walked out, and the woman followed him.

"We should just leave now," Elise said. "He already marked us down as here."

Rachel wished they could leave. "Yeah, except he saw us come in late. He'll know if we leave."

Elise sighed. "Yeah, you're probably right."

"I'm telling you, we need to get at least two kegs," a voice on the other side of Rachel said.

She and Elise stopped talking to eavesdrop.

It was Sean's friend Luke. Thanks to roll call, Rachel knew almost everyone's name in the class. She hadn't even seen him until now even though she should have known Luke would be there. He always sat with Sean.

"I don't know," said Sean. "I don't think everyone is going to drink beer. Especially the females."

"Let's ask them. Ladies?" Luke said.

Rachel and Elise turned to look at the two guys while trying to pretend they hadn't been snooping.

"What?" Elise said.

Luke leaned back, so he could look at them from behind Sean.

Luke was tall and muscular. He was the type of guy that Rachel was normally attracted to. Sean was short and skinny next to Luke, although Sean did have lean muscles. He was just a smaller guy all around. Luke had dark hair and dark eyes and looked to be of mixed heritage, although Rachel didn't know what. Compared to Luke, Sean's blond hair and blue eyes stood out. Blue eyes that were now staring at her.

Rachel purposely looked away to Luke since he was the one talking. Sean's gaze made her squirm in her seat.

"Do you ladies drink beer?" Luke asked. "Or would you prefer something else?"

Rachel looked to Elise, and they both shrugged.

Rachel turned back to the guys. "Don't know."

Sean and Luke frowned.

"What do you mean, *you don't know?*" Luke asked.

The girls exchanged looks again. It was a little embarrassing to admit that they hadn't been to any college parties yet. They had talked about them, but so far, they hadn't been invited to one.

Rachel looked at Elise, who rolled her eyes and said, "We haven't been to any parties yet, okay?"

"But..." Luke started.

Rachel looked back at him.

"But, what?" Elise asked.

"But...you're both hot."

Elise snorted. "As if that's the only reason to invite us to a party. If we were ugly, you wouldn't expect us to get invited?"

Luke was unfazed by Elise's comment. "Well, I didn't say that." He shrugged. "But you're more likely to be asked because you two *are* hot."

Elise made a sound of disgust.

Luke held up a hand. "Hey, I didn't make the rules." He narrowed his eyes at Elise. "Besides, you women are just as bad. You can't tell me that you'd throw a party and want all the dorks and ugos to show up."

Luke did have a point. Rachel knew she was more attracted to good-looking guys.

"You're right—to a point," she said. "Of course we're attracted to cute guys. But women are more open to other attributes besides looks. Overall, we're not as shallow as men."

"Ouch," Luke said.

Sean winced. "We're getting off topic," he said. "If you came to our party at our house on Saturday, would you drink beer, or would you want something else? Hard alcohol? Wine?"

Just then, the lady who had come in earlier reentered the room. "Class." She clapped her hands, and everyone quieted down. "Professor Drumming has a family emergency and won't be coming back to class today. You are all free to leave."

"Sweet," Elise said.

Rachel began putting her stuff away, grateful to get out of there.

She and Elise had to wait for Sean and Luke to get up and move before they could exit. The guys stood, and the girls followed.

Once they were in the hallway, Rachel and Elise started toward the nearest place to get coffee.

"Hey," Sean said behind them.

The two of them turned around.

"What?" Elise said.

"You never answered. What would you drink?"

Since it didn't matter and she didn't know why he was asking again, Rachel shrugged. "I'd drink whatever."

Elise must have thought the same thing as Rachel because she shrugged, too. "Yeah, it doesn't matter."

Luke grinned and elbowed Sean. "Told ya."

Sean raised a brow. "I guess we'll see." He looked at Luke. "Let's go."

The two guys spun around and began walking the other way.

Rachel told herself to bite her tongue, but she couldn't control her curiosity. "Wait."

The guys turned.

"What did you mean, *I guess we'll see?*"

"I guess we'll see on Saturday. Party starts at eight. See you then."

The two men turned back around and walked away, not sparing the girls another glance.

Rachel looked at her friend and roommate. "Are we going?"

"Hell yeah, we're going. That Luke guy might be a sexist pig, but this will be our first college party."

They grinned at each other, and like any other eighteen-year-olds, they squealed with excitement.

CHAPTER TWO

"Do I look okay?"

"Do *I* look okay?"

Rachel and Elise laughed at themselves and each other. Since this was their first college party, they were both a little nervous about looking like they belonged.

Rachel had thought about putting her light-brown hair up but then decided to wear it down around her shoulders in waves she had curled in. Her eyes were a boring hazel that she always tried to bring out with mascara and eye shadow. Sometimes, it worked; sometimes, they were still boring. Since the weather was still nice, Rachel opted for black lace shorts that showed off her still-tan legs. They were stylish and sexy yet comfortable. She paired those with a red V-neck shirt that would probably show off cleavage on anyone else, but on Rachel, it only showed skin. She still thought it was cute, and it went great with her shorts.

Elise wore her long blonde hair down, and her green eyes sparkled with excitement. She was dressed in a pair of skintight black capris that showed off her figure and a silky silver top that was modest yet sexy. At least, there was no cleavage for Elise either, although it was apparent that Elise had boobs, even without a V-neck shirt. On her feet were silver flats that matched her top.

Rachel had wanted to wear high heels so that there wouldn't be such a height difference between Elise's five-seven and her five-two, but Elise had pointed out that they might be standing all night. Knowing her friend was right, Rachel opted for a low heel instead. Two inches was two inches when you were short.

"We are way overthinking this," Elise said.

Rachel twirled around to look in her mirror. "Yeah, but there could be some really cute guys there." She watched Elise in the reflection as she turned back in her own mirror.

"I hope so. But I have to ask..."

Rachel spun around to look at her friend. "Have to ask what?" She really had no clue what Elise was thinking.

Elise met Rachel's eyes in the mirror as she picked up her eye shadow. "Does it matter if cute guys are there? Because you seem to be into Sean."

Rachel sighed. "You could tell, huh?"

Elise raised her brow. "I think my blind dog would be able to tell."

"You don't have a blind dog."

Elise laughed. "You know what I mean."

Rachel went back to her mirror and picked up her makeup. "Yeah, I'm attracted to him. *But* I don't want to be. Have you ever had that with anyone?"

"No," Elise answered way too fast.

Liar. Rachel chuckled.

She totally understood the feeling, so Rachel wasn't going to call Elise out on it, but she did wonder who the guy was that made her friend answer *no* way too fast.

"It's not like a crush where I daydream about him all the time or write my name with his last name. I honestly don't even think about him. Then, when I see him in class, it's like, *bam,* my heart starts beating fast, and my hormones go wild."

"What are you going to do about it?"

Rachel shrugged. "Nothing. Like I said, it's an unwanted attraction. Plus, he's never shown any interest in me, so I don't think I have to worry about anything."

"I guess we'll see tonight."

Rachel brushed some blush onto her cheeks. "I guess."

When Rachel and Elise reached the address on the piece of paper Sean had slipped onto Rachel's desk Thursday at class on his way to his usual seat, the party was already loud. Music and voices shouting could be heard from the street.

When the two of them reached the door, a guy neither girl had seen before stood there. "Five bucks each," he told them.

Rachel exchanged looks with Elise, who shook her head. They each had only brought the minimal things to the party —cell phone and dorm key. They didn't want to lose their purses, and neither of them had much pocket space.

"No one told us to bring money," Rachel explained.

The guy shrugged his shoulders. "Sorry, ladies. Maybe next time."

"But, but, Sean personally invited us," Rachel said.

"Sean and Luke," Elise added.

The guy chuckled. "Ladies, *everyone* is practically personally invited. Otherwise, no one would know to come."

Subtext: you two are not special.

"Can you just go ask him?" Rachel requested.

He snorted. "So, you two can sneak in? I don't think so."

Defeated, Rachel and Elise turned away, moving to the middle of the walkway where they stopped to talk.

"I guess we can go back and get some money," Elise suggested.

Sean and Luke lived all the way on the other side of campus from them, and they had walked there.

"That'll take, like, an hour. Plus, I don't have any cash. I was going to go to the ATM today, but I forgot. You? I can pay you back."

"Yeah, but—"

"Rachel, Elise, what are you two doing out there?" Sean called from the doorway.

Rachel blushed and was thankful it was dark outside. The streetlights weren't bright enough to show her complexion.

"We didn't bring cash to get in. We'll be back in about an hour!" Elise yelled back.

Sean waved his arm toward himself. "Get your asses in here."

"Awesome," Elise said.

Rachel sighed with relief. She really hadn't wanted to waste time in going to get money.

They made their way back up to the door.

When they reached it, Sean looked at them like they were crazy. "Why didn't you just come in? You two don't have to pay."

Rachel glanced behind Sean, but it didn't feel right to say anything.

"It was my fault, man. I didn't know," said the guy who wouldn't let them in.

"No problem, Liam. My bad. I didn't tell you I was waiting for them." To Rachel and Elise, he said, "Come on in, ladies."

Rachel looked around as she and Elise followed Sean. A few people were here and there on the main floor. Circling a big-screen TV were three couches with one couple talking on one and another making out on second. At the kitchen table, five people were playing a card game, taking drinks when the game called for it. But there weren't enough people to produce the loud noises they'd heard outside. That all seemed to be coming from the lower level.

Sean led them downstairs where the music was playing from one corner, loud enough to hear but not loud enough that people couldn't talk. Dozens of people were hanging around. Someone called Sean's name right away, and he split from them. Rachel suddenly felt awkward, and going by the look on Elise's face, she felt the same way.

What do we do now?

Movement off to one corner caught her eye, and Rachel

saw two girls from her Algebra class. She didn't know them well, but it was nice to see familiar faces.

Rachel motioned Elise to follow her. When they reached the other two girls, she made introductions. "Hi, Claire, Steph. This is my roommate, Elise. Elise, this is Claire and Steph. We have Algebra together."

The girls all said hi to one another.

"We're roommates, too. Two years now," Steph told Elise, taking a sip from her red Solo cup.

Rachel just realized that they were standing around, drinkless.

Elise must have realized the same thing because she asked, "Where do we get cups? And beer?"

Claire pointed behind them to the makeshift bar. "Keg is over there. We got cups when we paid at the door. Didn't you?"

Rachel and Elise shook their heads.

"We didn't pay," Rachel explained. "Sean let us in for free."

Claire and Steph exchanged looks.

"What?" Rachel asked.

Claire tilted her head and raised her brow so high, it almost hit her hairline. "Um...these guys don't just let anybody drink for free. They throw these parties to help pay their rent, and if they let all the girls get away with not paying, they wouldn't make half of their money. *Someone likes someone*," she said the last sentence in a singsong voice.

Elise directed her thumb at Rachel. "Sean likes Rachel."

Rachel sputtered because, for a moment, her heart skipped a beat. "No, he doesn't."

"Then, why did he let you in for free?" Steph asked.

"He let Elise in for free, too," Rachel pointed out. Although the part of her that liked Sean, whether she wanted to or not, did not like the fact that he might be after Elise. Sometimes, it sucked to be a girl.

Just then, Steph and Claire both smiled and snickered at whatever they saw behind Rachel and Elise. Two full cups appeared in front of Rachel and Elise. Rachel turned to see Sean standing behind her as she took one of the beers from his hand.

"Sorry, somebody needed help with the keg. Here are your drinks, ladies."

They each took a cup, and after his hands were empty, Sean moved to Rachel's side. He put his arm at her waist.

"Let me know if you need anything else, okay?" he said, giving her side a small squeeze.

"Will do," Elise said with a knowing smile.

Sean walked away, and Rachel looked at the three girls.

"Oh my God. Sean totally likes you. I knew it," Claire said. "I'm so jealous."

Rachel shrugged. She still wasn't convinced. Plus, there was the whole not-wanting-to-like-him thing even if that was changing by the second. "Eh...he's not really my type."

Steph raised her eyebrows. "Girl, *he* might not be your type, but in bed, he's everyone's type. You don't have to marry him. Just sleep with him."

Elise laughed. "What type is that?"

"The type that makes you come," Steph said.

"Isn't that kind of a given?" Rachel asked.

"Girl, who have you been dating?" Steph asked.

Rachel had dated a few guys in high school, but she'd only ever had sex with Kevin. And the orgasms had been hit or miss with her ex often not caring if she'd climaxed or not. "Okay, you're right. Men suck."

Everyone laughed.

"Well, not Sean. Apparently, he likes making women come."

Elise nodded enthusiastically. "I can get behind that." She elbowed Rachel. "I say, go for it, Rach."

Rachel frowned. "And you would know this because you slept with him?" she asked Steph. There was that stupid jealousy again.

Steph snorted. "Yeah, right. I wish. Sean doesn't sleep with just anyone."

Rachel looked over her shoulder to see Sean putting his arms around two girls who'd walked in from upstairs. She looked back at her friends. "Yeah, I don't know if I believe that."

"He's very sociable and a flirt, but he doesn't fuck everyone, like some guys. He might act like it, but I know plenty of girls who have been turned down by him," Steph said.

Rachel glanced at Sean again for a moment. As before, she understood he was good-looking, and she couldn't deny her unwanted attraction to him. But there were plenty of good-looking guys at their college. Sean was one in thousands.

"I don't get it. There are tons of hot guys at school. What's so special about Sean?"

Steph leaned into the circle and motioned for them to move closer. It was pointless since the music was so loud, but the rest of them leaned in, too, curious as to what Steph was going to tell them.

"Look, my cousin dated him last year for a couple of months before she transferred schools. She kind of has a big mouth. She said Sean was different from any other guy she'd ever slept with."

Rachel swallowed and tried not to react, but she couldn't deny that she was more than merely interested as to what Steph might say next.

"I already told you that he likes making women come, but I wasn't kidding or exaggerating. He gets off on it. Unlike most guys here who only care about getting their rocks off, Sean loves getting off the girl he's with. Like, he loves making her come over and over again. My cousin said that she almost passed out once."

Rachel felt her body flush from head to toe, and she had to pinch the inside of her arm to make herself not look at Sean again.

"Wow," Claire said. "I've heard that story more than once, but every time, it makes me hot."

Steph nodded. "Exactly. You need to hop on that, girl," she said to Rachel. "Pun intended."

CHAPTER THREE

Rachel had been at the party now for a couple of hours, and she and Elise had moved upstairs to play Asshole—or Presidents and Assholes, depending on whom you asked. For her first college party, it had started off a little rough, thinking they wouldn't get in, but it'd been all good from there.

They had just finished another game, all throwing their cards into a pile.

"I'm going to sit this one out," Rachel said. She was starting to really feel the effects of all the alcohol she'd drunk. If she didn't slow down a little, she'd be too drunk to walk home.

"Damn it," Elise said, grabbing all the cards and shuffling them. "And here I was, going to tell you to drink." Being the last player out of the game, she'd been named Asshole of the game, and while she dealt the cards, she got to tell anyone she wanted to drink, even the President.

"Sorry." Rachel smiled.

"Luke," Elise snapped. "Drink," she said with a sly glint in her eye.

Luke, who was very sexy in his own right, smirked at Elise and lifted his glass to his mouth. "You do realize who you're messing with, right?"

Luke had been the first one to get rid of all his cards, so therefore, he was the President. Once the game started and Elise was done dealing, Luke could make everyone at the table drink, but no one could make him drink. And being Asshole, everyone could make Elise drink. Rachel guessed that Luke was going to exact his revenge on her friend.

Elise smiled, cockiness in her eyes. "Yeah, I know. I just don't care."

A round of, "Ooh," was called out around the table, but Luke just laughed.

At that same moment, Sean came upstairs. Rachel had seen him on and off all night. He'd talked to her, gotten close, leaned in, and spoken next to her ear, even when he didn't have to, but he'd never really come out and hit on her. Still, Claire and Steph—and Elise, too, for that matter—had been insisting that he liked her. Yet she'd seen him chatting with other girls, too.

"Hey, Sean," Luke called.

"Yeah?" Sean asked, walking over to them now.

Luke grinned. "Will you grab me another beer?"

Sean shook his head with a smile. "Get your ass up, and get it yourself. I have to make sure the goods are safe," he said, turning and striding down the hall toward the bedrooms.

He'd hardly glanced at her just now, leaving her feeling confused.

Without a second thought, Rachel pushed her chair back and followed him. She was beyond curious at this point. Did Sean like her, or didn't he? And was he really a woman-pleaser in the bedroom? She really, really wanted to know that. All night, she'd been picturing Sean going down on her, and she was starting to get horny.

She found the room that Sean was in—it was the only one with the door half-open—and stepped in without being invited. Alcohol made her bold, and she'd seemed to forget the whole but-Sean's-not-my-type thing. Because the girls were right. A guy who liked giving orgasms was everyone's type. At least, for the night.

Sean was hunched down on the floor with his back to her. On his left was a dresser, and over to the right was a large bed.

Rachel cleared her throat.

Sean pivoted on the balls of his feet and looked over his shoulder. "Oh, hey." He set down whatever he'd been holding in his hand and closed the door on what now Rachel could see was a small safe. He stood and turned to face her. "What's up?"

Rachel stalked toward Sean. He might not be tall, but he was quite a bit taller than her, even with her two-inch heels on, and she had to look up at him.

"I have two questions for you."

Sean raised one eyebrow. "Shoot."

"Do you like me?"

Sean chuckled. "You don't beat around the bush, do you?"

Rachel shrugged. "Liquid courage." She stepped closer and put her hands on his chest. He was solid under her fingertips, and she wondered if he felt like that all over. "A few of my friends are convinced that you like me."

"But you're not so sure?"

"No."

One second, Rachel was standing in front of Sean, and the next, she was in his arms with her ass pushed against the edge of the dresser.

"What if I told you that your friends were right?" Sean asked, but he didn't give her a chance to answer because he kissed her.

Rachel melted into him. She hadn't been kissed by anyone since she and Kevin broke up, which was several months ago. And, damn...Sean was a good kisser. His hands slid up her bare legs and under her shorts. She was wearing a thong, which he quickly realized because he was soon cupping her naked butt.

Sean pulled her closer to him, and she felt his penis rub against her belly. She reached up and wrapped her fingers around him as best she could through his jeans. And, whoa, the man was not small everywhere.

Holy shit.

He felt bigger than her ex, who was six foot tall and broad-shouldered.

Sean broke their kiss, leaving the two of them panting. "Does that answer your question?"

"I...think so. Yes," Rachel said, still trying to catch her breath.

Sean studied her face. "What's your second question?"

Huh? Oh, yeah. She'd forgotten. She'd said she had two questions for him.

"I'm not normally one to partake in rumors," she started.

Sean lifted that eyebrow again.

She laughed. "Okay, so I lied. I'm a female. Of course I partake in rumors."

"What did you hear?" Sean asked, squeezing her ass.

She squeezed his thickness in response and said, "I heard that you liked to make women come."

Sean's smile faltered for a moment. It happened so fast that Rachel wasn't even sure if she'd really seen it.

"Ah...and I suppose you're the guinea pig who was voted to find out if it's true because they all decided that I liked you?"

Rachel was confused at first. "What? No. I'm here because I want to know. They have nothing to do with this."

She couldn't quite make out Sean's eyes in the dim light, but they looked resigned.

"Well, I suppose that's better than nothing, and as much as I should turn you away, I can't."

He kissed her again then, not giving her a chance to ask what he was talking about, and with the way Sean kissed, she soon forgot his cryptic words. She simply wanted him to keep kissing her.

His mouth was possessive and hot. He kneaded her ass as his mouth took control of their kiss. When she was pliant and jelly-like in his arms, his right hand slipped under the edge of her thong, and he trailed his fingers toward her front. Without any form of teasing, when he reached the spot, he pushed two fingers inside her and pressed his thumb directly on her clit. She felt the ring on his middle finger hit her opening, and it only made the whole experience hotter. She liked that single piece of jewelry he wore.

Rachel had to pull away from Sean's mouth as her knees buckled, and she shouted, "Holy fucking shit!" She had to grab on to his shoulders to brace herself because the dresser alone wasn't going to keep her upright.

It felt like he was rubbing his fingers against his thumb, and her body was trapped, caught, blessedly lucky to be in the middle. The pressure on her G-spot and clit were almost too much to bear. She alternated between standing on her tiptoes to try to put some space between them and pushing against his hand to make sure he wouldn't stop what he was doing.

She came with a loud cry, and she prayed the music blaring downstairs was enough to drown out the sound of her orgasm. Sean kissed her again, swallowing the rest of her moans, and she bucked against his hand. She couldn't remember coming so hard ever before in her life.

After her body settled and she was no longer trembling in his arms, Sean drew his hand from her shorts. She whimpered at the sudden emptiness in her vagina. She didn't want him to stop touching her. Ever.

Sean turned their bodies, so she faced toward the door, and he pulled his body away from hers to look into her face. He smiled, but it didn't quite reach his eyes.

"There's your answer, honey." With his left hand, he

playfully slapped her on the butt. "Now, get out of here. I need to finish up."

Rachel's body was still humming, and her mind was dazed, so she turned and walked away, doing as he'd directed. When she reached the door, she took one last look over her shoulder and saw Sean putting the fingers he'd used to make her come in his mouth, one by one, sucking the flavor of her off him.

It was probably the sexiest thing she'd ever seen. And, even though she'd gotten an excellent orgasm out of the whole encounter, it didn't sit right with her. She felt like she'd offended Sean or something, and she made a mental note to talk to him when he was done in his room.

Sean sensed more than heard Rachel walk away since the house was still filled with music and people.

He returned to the task of stacking the money they'd made on the party in his safe, working to keep his mind off of Rachel, but it was impossible.

He was trying really hard not to be cynical with their whole interaction, but he was disappointed. In her and himself.

He had no idea who had started the rumor that he liked handing out orgasms like they were Christmas presents, but somehow, it had been following him around since he was a freshman.

Although it wasn't a rumor if it was true, was it?

Because Sean liked pussy. And not like most men liked

pussy. Sure, he liked to stick his dick in it as much as the next guy, but he also loved the way it smelled, the way it tasted, the way it was so different from his own equipment. Apparently, everyone seemed to think this meant he had a kink.

Most of his friends either didn't like going down on a woman or did it just to get a blow job in return, but Sean loved eating a girl out. It was the most intimate place on a woman, and getting to put his mouth there was a privilege and a gift. He got hard from just thinking about it.

But then again, his dick was still stiff from bringing Rachel to climax.

Damn, he'd wanted to take her shorts off and shove his face between her legs. What little taste he'd had of her off his fingers wasn't enough.

But he'd refrained. The house party was still in full swing, and he couldn't leave Luke and his other two roommates to take care of everything without him. At some point, they'd have to start kicking people out and do a preliminary cleanup before they went to bed.

However, he knew, if he'd really wanted to take her down to his bed and spend a good hour making her come, he'd have done it. No, what had really stopped him was the fact that she'd sought him out because of the stupid rumor. Not because she was interested in him as a person.

Someone needed to tell the women of the world not to kiss and tell instead of always directing that statement toward men.

Sean shut the safe door and twisted the knob to lock it. He stood and swiped his hand down his face. Suddenly, he was exhausted and just wanted to be done with tonight.

He left his room and shut and locked the door. One could never be too careful with drunk partygoers. He exited the hall and saw Rachel sitting at the kitchen table again. Without drawing attention to himself, he slipped down the stairs and avoided her detection.

CHAPTER FOUR

Rachel woke with the foggiest brain and a headache that put all others to shame. She groaned as she rolled over. She wanted to stay sleeping, but her bladder demanded that she got up.

"Oh God," she muttered. If this was what going to a house party was like, she was never going to go to another.

She snorted at herself. *Yeah, right.* That wasn't going to happen. She couldn't even remember getting home the night before, but she doubted that would stop her when the next party invite rolled around.

She slowly opened her eyes to orientate herself, only to comprehend that she was not in her bed or in her dorm. It took her a second to realize she was in Sean's room.

Her eyes widened as she went from half-asleep to fully awake. She glanced over to the other side of the bed.

Empty. And, going by the covers pulled to the top, it had been that way all night.

She slowly lifted the comforter.

She was fully clothed; the only things missing were her shoes. She patted herself down just to make sure, and yep, she was still wearing her bra. Ugh, she hated sleeping in her bra.

She slowly sat up so as not to jar her head, and she saw a bottled water and a container of ibuprofen on the nightstand. That was when she remembered how the night had ended.

After leaving Sean's room, she'd gone and played cards again to wait for him to come out. She hadn't realized he'd left his room and gone immediately downstairs. Before she had known it, she'd drunk way too much.

Elise had left a little earlier and wanted Rachel to go with, but she had been determined to talk to Sean and apologize for whatever she'd done to upset him. Why she hadn't just gone back to his bedroom to find him, she didn't know.

Alcohol had made her bold but not the brightest person in the room.

When she'd finally found Sean, she'd been beyond intoxicated, and she'd totally botched her apology. It'd come out as gibberish, she was sure, and Sean had taken her to his room, laid her down, slipped off her shoes, and covered her up. He'd brought her water and medicine for the morning and left her to sleep.

He hadn't even kissed her before leaving.

Rachel grabbed the meds, shook three out, and downed them with the entire bottle of water.

She didn't know when her feelings for Sean had changed, but they had. Two days ago, she hadn't wanted to be attracted to him. This morning, she was bereft that he hadn't kissed her good night.

She was such a girl.

Grabbing her shoes off the floor, she went in search of the first free bathroom to empty her bladder and maybe clear her head, too.

The hallway was quiet when she opened the door, and she slipped into the bathroom a door down from Sean's room. She tried to be as quiet as possible, but she was clumsy after drinking the night before.

She dropped a shoe, knocked over a vial of cologne, and was unable to run the water in the sink on anything other than full blast. And let's not forget, the tsunami that sounded when she flushed the toilet.

She winced as she exited, but everything was still quiet. *Whew.*

She tiptoed out into the living room, intending to head straight to the front door, but she glanced over at the semi-circle of couches and saw Sean fast asleep.

He was lying on his back with one arm thrown over his head, hanging off the side of the couch, and the other on his bare stomach. His beautiful, bare stomach. Rachel had assumed that Sean was hiding muscles under his T-shirt, especially after touching him last night, but she'd had no idea he was so ripped.

She sucked in a breath. *Wow.*

He was a smaller, slim guy, but that did not take away from the fact that his pecs were well defined. She wanted to run her fingertips over his eight-pack to see if his muscles moved when she touched him.

He had two tattoos on his left side—one on his rib cage and one on his hip. What really surprised her was, his left nipple was pierced. Somehow, she'd missed that when she caressed his chest the night before. It was sexy on him.

He had one leg sticking out of the blanket that covered his lower half, and she saw he was wearing gray sweatpants. She was bummed. She knew he probably wouldn't be sleeping naked in his living room, but she'd been hoping he was wearing only his underwear, so she could have gotten to see an outline of his impressive package.

Jeez, what is wrong with me?

She had gone from avoiding him to wanting to see his dick. She was not a nice person. Sean had been nothing but a gentleman to her, minus the hands-up-her-shorts thing, and she was trying to get a peek at his junk while he slept.

Filled with guilt, she cautiously approached him. She'd wake him only to say a short apology, and then she'd go home. She set her shoes on the large square coffee table and placed her hand on his shoulder.

"Sean," she whispered. "Sean, wake up a sec, please."

One eye opened just enough to peek at her. "What's up?" he asked.

Then, he closed his eye and fell back asleep; she could tell by his deep breathing.

She sighed. "Sean," she said again. She added in a shoulder squeeze.

The same eye opened.

"I need to tell you, I'm sorry."

"Okay." Again, his eye closed, and his breathing deepened.

She'd never had to work so hard to apologize to someone. She shook him this time. "Sean, please listen to me."

Both eyes opened to tiny slits. "Later," he said. He grabbed her and pulled her down next to him. Her back was to him, and he tucked her to his side, spooning her and wrapping his body around hers. "Go back to sleep. We'll talk later."

Rachel's body hummed at the nearness and warmth of his body. There was no way she was going to go back to sleep, but now, she felt guilty for waking him. And there was no way she'd be able to slip from his arms without fully rousing him from his sleep.

Resigned to hanging out there for a while, she closed her eyes and snuggled back against Sean. It had been a long time since she got to sleep next to a man. She might as well enjoy it for a bit.

He smelled and felt delicious, and before she knew it, she was asleep again too.

When Rachel woke again, she was alone on the couch. She glanced around and didn't see anyone, but she could hear noises coming from the lower level.

She went downstairs to find Sean but only saw Luke and two other guys. Someone had told her that Sean and Luke had two other roommates, and Rachel assumed these were the guys. The three of them were picking up garbage and cleaning up.

"Rachel," Luke said when he saw her, a huge grin on his face.

She ignored whatever the smile might mean. "Is Sean

around?" she asked.

Luke's smile faded. "He left," he said as if he didn't want to admit it.

"Do you know when he'll be back?"

Luke glanced at his roommates, who grimaced and shrugged. Luke looked back at her. "Tomorrow."

"Tomorrow?"

"Yeah, he went home for the rest of the weekend. Sorry."

Rachel thought about his comment for a moment. Luke thought she and Sean had had sex, and then Sean had ditched her.

"Oh, it's okay. He let me sleep in his bedroom while he slept on the couch. I just wanted to thank him."

Luke looked relieved at this news. "I'll tell him."

"Thanks," Rachel said and headed back upstairs. She grabbed her shoes, slipped them on, and headed for her dorm.

When she unlocked the door to her and Elise's room, she was disappointed to see Elise was still asleep. She'd been hoping that her friend would be up and available to talk.

Knowing whatever she had to say could wait, Rachel grabbed her shower supplies and headed to the bathroom. Maybe washing away the smell of alcohol and the party would help clear her head.

When she returned to her room, Elise was awake.

"What happened last night? You didn't come home," her roommate asked.

"I got too drunk to walk home, and I slept in Sean's bed."

"Ooh," Elise said excitedly.

"Alone. He slept on the couch."

"Oh." This time, her friend's voice was flat with disenchantment.

"Yeah," Rachel agreed.

"So, nothing else happened?"

Rachel told Elise about finding Sean in his room, them kissing, and him touching her until she exploded. About how she'd slept alone and how Sean was gone when she woke up.

"I think I offended him or something. He changed for a split second when I mentioned the rumors Steph and Claire had told us. But, when I tried to apologize, he kind of brushed me off."

"I'm sure it'll be okay. Maybe he doesn't think you need to apologize, and that's why he didn't really respond."

Rachel wasn't sure. "I don't know."

"You'll see on Tuesday. Everything will be back to normal."

Elise was right. Everything went back to normal the next week. Rachel and Elise sat in their normal spots in the middle of the room, and Sean and Luke took their usual seats off to the left toward the front. Sean made no effort to speak to her.

Rachel no longer had the boldness of alcohol to give her the courage to approach Sean on her own, but she found an excuse to stick around outside of the classroom after she and Elise got out before the guys.

Rachel straightened from her kneeling position on the floor where she'd been looking in her bag for her money for coffee. She'd been watching for Sean out of the corner of her eye, and when he was almost out, she stood and threw her backpack over her shoulder.

She pretended to be surprised to see it was him and opened her mouth to ask him about the rest of the weekend, but when Sean saw her and Elise, he simply said, "Ladies," with a nod and continued on.

Luke said hello, and the two were off.

Rachel wouldn't speak to Sean again for two months.

CHAPTER FIVE

I t was December now in Minnesota, and Rachel and Elise shrugged off all their winter gear as they took their seats in World Religions. As always, Rachel looked over at Sean, who rarely ever spared her a glance anymore.

The worst part was, she didn't think he was being coy or playing hard to get. He'd pretty much lost interest in her while her awareness of him had increased tenfold.

He was constantly on her mind. He was in her thoughts, her dreams, and her fantasies when she touched herself. She'd gone from not wanting him to having a full-blown crush.

She tried not to think about him. She'd even gone on a couple of dates. But the guy was not Sean. And she didn't even know the guy that well.

She was seriously considering therapy at this point.

Thankfully, the fall semester would be over at the end of

the month, and she'd no longer have class with him. Of course, that also made her sad.

"Okay, class, for part of your final, we're going to do a project," Professor Drumming announced to the class after taking roll call. "I find it breaks up the monotony of taking tests all the time."

There were a few moans around the class.

"We've covered the major religions in class, but there are over four thousand religions in the world. You get to pick any of the religions we haven't covered here to do your report on. And, just because I'm a nice guy, you get to work on this with a partner."

The class murmured sounds of relief, and Rachel looked at Elise. She already knew whom her partner would be.

The professor held up his hands to quiet them. "Wait, wait. I'm not that nice of a guy because you're not going to pick your partners. At least, not the way you think."

This time, Rachel groaned with the rest of her classmates. It was so hard to share a grade with someone you didn't know. And finding time to get together always seemed like a challenge because no one wanted to spend their free time with a practical stranger.

"This sucks," Elise complained.

"Tell me about it."

"So, class, there are thirty-two of you in here. We're going to make eight groups of four. And, of those four, you get to pair off." Professor Drumming grinned. "See, I told you that you'd get to work with a partner."

"How generous," Rachel muttered.

"Ass," Elise said.

The class began counting off from one to eight. After they were finished, Rachel went to find out who else was in group five. She just prayed she'd be paired up with someone who would pull their own weight.

When she got to the spot with the other fives, only two others were there. A guy named Ryan and a girl named Annie. Rachel hadn't spoken to the other two students at all, but she'd heard them answer questions in class, so with any luck, she'd end up with one or the other.

"Hey," Rachel said.

"Hey," Annie said. "I hope you don't mind, but we've already decided to be each other's partner."

"Oh. Okay," she said. Rachel didn't really know how else to respond.

"We have another class together," Annie tried to explain, obviously feeling bad for excluding Rachel.

Rachel smiled. "No, it's no problem. I understand." She looked around as people were still getting up and moving to their respective groups. "I wonder who I'll wind up with."

"Me," a voice said from behind her.

Rachel turned to see Sean standing there.

She didn't know if she should be excited or nervous.

There was a knock at Rachel's dorm door.

"Elise, will you please answer it?" she asked from underneath the blankets pulled over her head.

The only answer she received was another knock on the door.

Pushing down her comforter, Rachel scanned the room. Empty.

Damn it.

She was tired, and she didn't feel like facing anyone. She'd stayed up late the night before to study for her Biology final on Monday. Instead of going out, partying, or having fun, she'd taken care of her obligations, being a good student. Her reward was supposed to be sleeping in this morning.

She hoped whoever was on the other side of that door was tough because she was cranky and in no mood for bullshit.

Rachel ripped the door open to tell the person who had dared to knock on her door to go away, only to find Sean standing there. "Oh, crap."

"Good morning," he said, pushing past her and dropping his bag on the ground.

Rachel swung the door closed and plopped down into one corner of the couch. "No, it's not. Sorry, I forgot we were supposed to meet," she said with a yawn.

Sean sat down on the opposite side. "Long night?" he asked.

Despite her tiredness, Rachel studied him. He'd asked the question casually. Almost too casually.

"Yes," was her only answer. She wanted to see how he reacted.

His lips tightened but only for a moment. "Have fun?"

Happy with her little test, Rachel answered honestly, "No. I was up until two or three, studying for Biology." She snuggled down into the sofa to get more comfortable. "It was the exact opposite of fun."

He grimaced. "Sorry. Do you want to reschedule? We're almost done. I don't see us needing to meet more than one more time."

"Nah. I'm already up. Might as well finish this thing."

Sean raised his brow. "You sure? You look like you're going to fall back asleep."

Rachel sighed and stood to grab her stuff. "No, I'm up."

It was a good thing she was tired though because she just realized that she was with Sean in her flannel pajamas with bedhead and no makeup. However, she could be standing naked in front of him, and he probably wouldn't care.

Despite his brief appearance of unhappiness upon thinking Rachel was out late, he had made no moves of any sort the last two weeks. Not even any flirting. He'd clearly gotten over whatever he first felt for her.

But, just in case, Rachel grabbed a mint from her desk and popped it into her mouth.

"Now, where'd we leave off?" she asked as she sat next to him.

A couple of hours later, they were putting the finishing touches on their report.

"Ah...it feels good to be done with something," Rachel said. "We'd better get an A on this thing, or I'm going to egg Drumming's house."

"In winter?"

"Hell yeah. Frozen eggs. It'd be a bitch to get off."

Sean laughed and packed up his stuff. "Do you want to get a late breakfast?"

Rachel's eyes widened at his question. But she soon realized he only meant as classmates, not like a date or anything.

She looked down at her appearance, so he couldn't see her disappointment. "I think I need to shower and get dressed first. Can you wait fifteen minutes?"

"I can. But, for the record, you don't need to shower. You always look good."

Rachel jerked her head up, and her mouth hung open.

"What?" he said with a laugh.

She licked her lips. "I had no idea you felt that way."

With furrowed brows, he said, "I seem to recall an occurrence in my bedroom that would say otherwise."

"But...but..." She was at a loss for words. "You haven't done anything about it since."

"That's because I found out you were just trying to get an orgasm out of me." He shrugged. "Some guys might like being used for sex, but I'm not one of them."

This time, she was confused. "I didn't want to use you for sex."

"Didn't you?" he asked.

She had to think hard about that night. It was a couple of months ago now, and she'd been drinking that night. "Is this because I told you what my friends had said about you...how you liked getting women off?"

"Yes."

She snapped her fingers. "I knew something had bothered you that night. Why didn't you let me apologize?"

He laughed in disbelief. "I don't want or need your apologies."

She cocked her head. "Then, what do you want?"

"You."

"But..."

"I wanted you to come to my room because of me, not because of some rumor."

Rachel got up on her knees and swung one over his lap. She ran her fingers over his face. His blue eyes looked so serious, as if the next thing out of her mouth would be a tipping point.

"I did come to your room because of you. I already liked you. That rumor just gave me one more reason to approach you. But it had nothing to do with how I already felt."

Sean grabbed her face and pulled her mouth down to kiss her. He was an even better kisser than she remembered. God, he knew just what to do with his lips and tongue.

He pulled away and grinned at her. With a slap on her ass, he said, "Go. You have fifteen minutes."

CHAPTER SIX

"How do I look?" Rachel asked Elise. She had on a red shirt and a black skirt with nylons because it was January in the Midwest. And, on her feet, she wore red four-inch heels to give herself some height.

Her roommate gave her two thumbs-up. "Great. He won't know what hit him."

"God, I hope so." Rachel glanced at the clock. "Is it seven yet?"

Elise chuckled from the couch. "Nervous?"

"Yes, and I don't know why."

"Well, it is your first date," Elise said. "And you've had all break to think about it."

"Anticipation's a bitch."

Elise laughed.

Rachel had gone to have breakfast with Sean after they finished their World Religions assignment. When they had finished eating, he'd brought her back to her dorm room, and after a thorough kiss at her door, he'd taken off. But he had made her promise to go out with him. As if he'd really have to force her.

But then it was finals week and then winter break. Rachel's mom, stepfather, and little sister lived in the Minneapolis–St. Paul area, but they'd gone to visit her step-grandparents a couple hours from the Twin Cities over the holidays. And Sean had gone home to visit his family a couple of hours away. So, while the two had talked on the phone quite a few times over the break, this was their first official date. Breakfast didn't count in her book.

Rachel was nervous as hell. It was silly because she already knew he liked her, yet she couldn't stop feeling anxious.

"Did you pack a toothbrush in your purse?" Elise asked.

"*What? No.*" Rachel pretended to be outraged. "Just kidding. I have a toothbrush and a change of underwear."

"And do you have your lipstick?" Elise asked.

"Check."

"Your cell phone in case you need to call me?"

"Check."

"Toothbrush, yes. Toothpaste, just in case?"

"Check."

"Condoms?"

"Check, check, check," Rachel answered with a nod.

"Check, check, check?"

"Condom one, condom two, and condom three." Rachel grinned. "Just in case."

Elise laughed. "Smart girl. Do you think you'll have sex tonight?"

"I hope so, but I have no idea," Rachel said with a shrug. "I guess we'll find out."

There was a knock at the door, and Rachel's heart sped up even faster than it had already been beating.

"Good luck," Elise said, standing up and hugging her roommate.

"Thanks." Rachel turned and opened the door.

Sean whistled the second he saw her, and she blushed.

"You don't look too shabby yourself."

He was wearing a nice pair of dark jeans and a black henley shirt with a dark gray jacket for the cold.

"I hope I'm not too dressed up."

Sean's eyes were on her legs. "No way," he said.

Rachel laughed, and he looked at her.

He smiled without an ounce of shame. "You ready?"

"Yes," she told him. She gave Elise one last wave and closed the door.

Rachel had been worried about having an awkward silence, but they talked easily with one another on the way to the restaurant.

"Did you have a good Christmas?" Sean asked her.

"It was good. We went to my grandparents'."

"Mom's or dad's?"

"My dad. Technically, he's my stepdad, so they're my stepgrandparents, but I call them Grandma and Grandpa. My birth dad left when I was one."

"I'm sorry."

She chuckled. "It's okay. I don't remember it. And I have a pretty great stepdad."

Her stepfather, whom she called and considered her real dad, was the reason that she had turned out sane.

After her birth father had left, her mother had done a lot of man-hopping. And not always with the best guys. Growing up, she and her mother had needed to move around a lot, oftentimes with no place to go to right away. That was, until her mother found a new man. Then, her mother would catch the guy cheating or he'd kick Rachel and her mom out after growing sick of her or the cops would be after him or any number of scenarios before they'd have to move again.

Rachel's only saving grace was that the Minneapolis–St. Paul area was big, so they never had to move far, and she hadn't had to switch schools often. Then, her mother had met Ralph Garwood. They'd gotten married when Rachel was eight, and her life had changed for the better. No more loser boyfriends and no more worrying about where they'd be living in a year.

"He would've adopted me," Rachel continued, "but my mom was never able to find my dad to sign the papers. On my eighteenth birthday, I legally changed my last name to his. What about your parents? How was your Christmas?"

"Still married. Christmas was the same as usual. We had it at my parents' place, and the night ended with my brothers and me getting in a wrestling match."

Rachel laughed. "How many brothers do you have?"

"Two older. Not only am I the youngest, but I'm also the smallest. I've had to live my life being called the runt."

"I understand how you feel. My sister is nine years younger than me and is already taller than me."

"It sometimes sucks, being small."

Rachel grabbed his hand, interlacing their fingers. "You're not small to me."

Sean looked away from the road to smile at her.

She leaned in close to him and whispered, "And I already know a very specific part of you is not small in any way." She made sure he looked at her before she directed her eyes at his crotch.

He groaned. "I really wish I weren't driving right now, so I could kiss you."

Rachel sat back in her seat, grinning with satisfaction.

The restaurant Sean had chosen had dim lighting, and they were seated in a corner. It was still out in the open, but the position gave them a little more privacy than if they were sitting out in the middle.

The hostess had sat them down, and within seconds, their server came over to take their drink orders. Since neither of them were twenty-one, they settled for water.

"When's your birthday?" she asked him, picking up a menu.

"End of next month."

"And you'll be twenty-one?"

Sean smiled. "Finally. Although I'm not as excited as some people are to turn twenty-one. You?"

"Mine was in November. I just turned nineteen, so I have two years to go."

"It'll go fast," he assured her, but she doubted it.

They looked over the menus, and when the server came back with their waters, they ordered dinner.

After the waitress left, Sean leaned in close. They were sitting perpendicular to each other at the square table, so he didn't have to go far to get close. "Have I told you that you look great tonight?"

She pretended to think about it. "I think you just whistled."

"My apologies. You look good enough to eat." He groaned. "I wish I could do just that. Or at least touch you."

She leaned in, too. "And where do you want to touch me?"

He put his hand on her leg. "Here but higher. I want to feel how silky and wet you are. I've thought about it every day since that night in my bedroom. It wasn't nearly enough."

Rachel sucked in a breath through her mouth. "And why can't you touch me there?" she taunted him.

He growled. "I'm very tempted, believe me. But we're in public. Plus"—he pinched her nylons between his fingers and snapped it against her leg—"you have a nice barrier here."

She shrugged. "It's cold outside." She looked around the room. "I'm going to use the restroom before our food gets here."

Sean nodded, slipped his hand from her leg, and sat back in his chair. As she stood and grabbed her purse, she watched him adjust himself in his jeans.

When he caught her watching, he smirked.

She quickly used the women's restroom. It took her a little longer to do what she wanted in the tiny stall, but in the end, it was worth it. She gave herself a once-over in the mirror to make sure her makeup looked good and her hair was still in an updo before she went back to the table.

She sat back down just as the food was arriving. While Sean had his attention on the server and his steaming plate, Rachel opened her purse and pushed a present into Sean's jeans pocket.

"Everything look good?" the waitress asked.

"Yes, it looks delicious," Rachel answered honestly.

They dug into their food when, suddenly, Sean shifted and frowned. "Did you put something in my pocket?" he asked.

Rachel laughed. "Yes. You just now noticed?"

"I noticed before, but I wasn't really paying much attention at the moment. I'm a growing boy; my mind was on the food at that particular second."

"So, if you could have an endless supply of food or sex, whichever way you desire it, for the rest of your life, what would you choose?" Rachel asked as Sean slouched in his seat to reach in his pocket.

When he realized what he was holding in his hand, he quickly shoved it back in his jeans. He shifted in his seat and moved his chair closer to her. "You put your thong in my pants pocket."

"Yes." She tilted her head and blinked innocently. "Why? Is that bad?"

He laughed in disbelief. "You know it's not." He lowered his voice. "How did you do it?"

"Oh, didn't I tell you? I'm wearing thigh-high nylons and a garter belt." She pushed a piece of food into her mouth and sucked on the fork. "You're free to touch me however you want."

She squeaked when Sean pulled her chair closer and positioned her leg over his lap. He pushed one finger and then two deep inside her.

Rachel dropped her fork with a clang and grabbed the edge of the table. "Holy shit," she panted. When she looked up and saw that some people were questionably eyeing her, she gave them a weak smile and rubbed her stomach as if it hurt. "Sorry."

Thank God the tablecloth was long, so no one could see what Sean was doing to her, which was the same sort of thing he'd done in his bedroom.

How did he know how to touch her like that already? She'd dated her ex for over a year, and he'd never been able to bring her to orgasm so fast.

"Holy shit, I'm going to come."

"Not yet," Sean said and pulled his hand away. He brought his fingers to his lips and sucked on them, one by one, like that night in his bedroom.

Rachel didn't even see their server approaching their table until she was touching the table with her hand.

"How is everything?" she asked.

Sean drew the tip of his finger from his lips. "Delicious," he said without a hint of a double meaning or sexual innuendo.

CHAPTER SEVEN

S ean tried to act cool and collected throughout the rest of dinner, but he couldn't wait to get Rachel home and naked.

She'd shocked him when he discovered that she'd slipped her underwear in his pocket. He loved that she was so bold. Most college girls were timid, or if they weren't, they were afraid to show their real selves in fear of being judged. But Rachel just did what she wanted.

It was fucking sexy as hell.

The fact that she'd let him finger her in a crowded restaurant? Well, that made her the most desirable woman on campus, if not the world.

And, right now, she was his.

Sean paid the bill while Rachel squirmed in her seat. He knew he'd left her wanting, but he remembered the way she'd come in his room. She had been loud and hadn't held back. He hadn't wanted her to be embarrassed if others gawked at her. Plus, he was selfish. He wanted her orgasms all to himself. Also, a little anticipation never hurt anyone.

He adjusted his hard-on in his pants before he stood. Then, he helped Rachel put on her coat before he put on his own.

Once in his car, neither of them said much, so Sean felt the need to clear something up. "Rachel?"

She looked over at him. "Yeah?"

He looked away from the road to meet her eyes. "You're coming back to my place. We're going to finish what we started at dinner."

She didn't respond, so he put his hand on her leg and pushed her skirt up until he reached the top of the nylons. He played with the straps that connected them to her garter belt. "I think I'm going to have to keep these on you while I fuck you with my mouth. I want to feel them as you squeeze my head when you come all over my face."

"You think very highly of yourself," she tried to say with an air of indifference, but he heard her voice catch.

He trailed his fingers higher until he reached the outside of her pussy lips. She was wet, and he wanted to be home. Now. He played around for a second before making a beeline for her clit.

Rachel practically jumped off her seat. Thankfully, her seat belt kept her in place as Sean rubbed her engorged nub.

"Nah," he finally answered her question. "The thing about life is, you need to know what you're good at and what you're not. And, sweetheart, I already *know* I'm good at making you come."

When they reached Sean's house, Rachel was ready to vault from the car and run to the door. Too bad she could hardly walk.

The ache between her legs was at a ten. Her clit was swollen, and her pussy was so wet that she could feel it on her legs, thanks to Sean holding her underwear in his pocket. Sean wouldn't let her come in the car. He'd kept playing with her, bringing her close and then backing off before she could actually explode.

Sean came around to her side and opened her door. Such a gentleman. She stared at his fingers as he closed the passenger door. His fingers that had been between her legs. He was a kinky gentleman.

"Why the smile?" he asked her.

"Just thinking about you."

He pulled her close. "Good," he said and kissed her.

About the time she was ready to hump his leg outside in his driveway, he released her.

"Let's go inside." He put his hand on her back and led her around to the side door.

They entered the kitchen, and Sean went directly to the fridge. He grabbed a bottle of water, leaned against the counter, and drank the whole thing in one long drink. When he was finished, he took a deep breath and wiped his mouth with the back of his hand. "Sorry. I need to hydrate before we get started. Do you want anything?"

Yeah. An orgasm. "Fuck no," she answered.

Sean laughed, but she was serious. She wanted to get this particular party started.

His expression changed when she didn't laugh, too. He screwed the cap onto the water bottle and threw it toward the garbage in the corner, making it in the basket. "Okay." He pushed himself away from the counter and took a step toward her. "Go to my room. Take off all your clothes. Lie on the bed, and wait for me."

She nodded with a smile and turned to do as he'd said.

He grabbed her hand before she got too far, and she looked at him over her shoulder.

"I almost forgot. Leave the nylons and garter belt on." He let go of her hand and swatted her on the ass.

She noticed that he sure liked doing that to her. She chuckled. She liked it, too.

As she walked down the hall to his bedroom, she couldn't help but feel sexy and desirable. When she reached his room, she saw the same lamp was on that had been on the night of the party. She closed the door behind her and began to strip.

She kicked her shoes into the corner and pulled her dress over her head. She looked around, trying to figure out where to set it. She folded it up and decided to put it on his dresser. She'd already removed her underwear at the restaurant, so now, she was left in her nylons and garter belt.

She turned toward the bed, taking her to her next big decision. What to do now while she waited. *Stand here? Lie on the bed? On top? Under the covers?*

She'd just put one knee on the bed with the intention to crawl to the middle when she heard the door open.

She started to put her leg down and turn around when she heard Sean groan.

"Do not move."

Rachel wiggled her ass a little in response.

Sean groaned again.

The door closed, and she heard him approach. His clothed body pressed up against her mostly naked one, and there was no mistaking the bulge in his pants. She reached around and squeezed him as he rubbed his hands down her body.

He moved her hair off her shoulder and kissed her nape. It started with light pecks but soon turned into hot, slick open-mouthed kisses.

Now, it was her turn to groan.

Sean grabbed her hair and gently pulled her head back against him as he continued to suck and lick her. Rachel's neck was definitely one of her biggest erogenous zones, and she was burning up inside.

He slipped his fingers between her legs and played with her wet folds. "Damn. Love how wet you are." He stepped back and gave her a small push forward. "Get up on the bed on your hands and knees."

Rachel did as he'd said and made sure to open her legs nice and wide to give Sean a great view.

She looked over her shoulder, and Sean licked his lips with a smile.

He lifted his chin. "Further, babe."

She crawled forward until she was just past the middle of the bed. She looked down between her legs to watch as Sean lay down on the bed on his back and scooted up until his head was underneath her. He gripped her hips in his hands and lowered her pelvis until her pussy hit his lips.

His mouth was scorching, and his tongue licked every inch of her vagina, except the part where she really wanted him. He repeatedly bypassed her clit until she was seconds away from letting her knees go and rubbing her pussy against his face until she finally came.

But he must have sensed that she was on the verge of taking matters under her own control because he lightly flicked his tongue over her swollen bud. That was all it took for Rachel to combust. She clenched her fists in the comforter underneath her and howled out a noise that sounded more like a wounded animal than a woman coming. She didn't care though because the orgasm was that good.

Sean clutched her hips in his hands to keep her from falling on him, probably smothering him with her body. When she began to feel like herself again rather than a big blast of molecules floating in the sky, Sean lowered her pelvis. This time, instead of teasing her, he went straight for the bull's-eye.

She made a halfhearted attempt to pull away because she was super sensitive but gave in as sensitivity turned into pleasure. She let Sean try to coax her toward another climax because it felt good, not because she would get off again. She'd tried to have multiple orgasms with her ex-boyfriend and on her own but to no avail.

So, when white-hot flashes of desire coursed over and through her body, Rachel cried out in surprise as much as pleasure. There was no way her legs were going to hold her up much longer, and she used her few functioning brain cells to roll away from Sean and collapse on the bed.

He crawled up beside her and looked down at her face.

"I didn't know I could do that."

The corner of his mouth turned up. "Do what?"

"Come. Twice."

Sean brought his face close to hers until their mouths were practically touching. "Why don't we see if we can make it three times?"

Rachel's eyes grew wide with doubt, but then he kissed her as he cupped her breast and thumbed her nipple. By the time he slipped his fingers between her wet folds again, she was more than eager to let him try.

CHAPTER EIGHT

R achel was lying on Sean's bed as she watched him get ready for the night, feeling sad. "This sucks."

He looked over his shoulder as he pulled a crew neck shirt from his closet hanger. "I don't have to go. I'm more than willing to stay home."

She sat up and shook her head. "No way. It's your birthday. You're only twenty-one once, and you're not staying home to sit here with my sick ass."

Rachel had planned big things for Sean's twenty-first birthday. She'd gotten a fake ID so that she could go out with him and his friends, and then she was going to bring him home and finally make love to him.

They'd been together since their first date, almost two months now, but they still hadn't had actual sex. Despite not wanting to date so soon and never rushing into a relationship, thanks to her mother, she couldn't stay away from Sean.

Steph and Claire were right; Sean loved making Rachel come over and over. The two times she'd gone down on him, she'd practically had to beg him to let her return the favor. She was living every woman's fantasy.

But she wanted to take it to the next level. She wanted to come with Sean inside her, and she wanted to feel him come, too.

Unfortunately, a virus had swept hard through their campus, and Rachel hadn't been able to escape the sickness. So, instead of getting to spend tonight with her new boyfriend while he celebrated one of his biggest birthdays and then coming home and blowing his mind, she was going to be lying in bed, blowing her nose.

"At least Elise is sick, too. We can be pathetic together tonight."

"That was nice of you to give her your sickness."

"When I walked out the door this morning, I told her never to say I didn't give her anything."

Sean laughed. "And what was her response?"

"I believe she told me to go fuck myself." Rachel shrugged with a smile. "I'm just glad I got to come over and see you today."

Rachel was on the mending side of her illness and felt better today than yesterday and yesterday more than the day before. Her fever was gone, but she was not one hundred percent. There was no way she could go out drinking. She was probably going to fall asleep before ten as it was. It was barely eight, and she was already tired. At least she'd felt good enough to venture out of her dorm room to see Sean for a little while. She'd showered and tried to make herself look as pretty as possible, but it was hard when she still had puffy eyes and a red nose.

Sean pulled his shirt over his head and came to sit beside her. "About that."

"Yes?"

"I want you to stay here tonight." He put his hand on her cheek. "I want you here, in my bed, when I get home."

"Are you sure? I already feel bad that I came over. Your roommates are going to hate me if they get sick."

He kissed her forehead. "I don't care. It's my birthday, and my present is coming home to find you in my bed."

She smiled. "Okay. But I want you to know that I'll be fully clothed with a bad case of bedhead."

Sean shook his head in mock suffering. "I guess that's a sacrifice I'm willing to make."

She pushed him until he fell back against the bed, so she could lay her head on his chest. She tried to breathe in his scent, but her nose was still plugged, and she gave up, disappointed. "Will you promise me, you'll be careful? No alcohol poisoning, okay?"

For someone who hadn't wanted to get into a serious relationship, she sure had fallen fast for this guy. She couldn't quite say for sure that she was in love with Sean, but she knew she was headed there. And she was pretty sure he felt the same about her.

He rubbed his hand up and down her arm. "I promise, I'll be careful. I already told the guys not to kill me."

Rachel snorted. She doubted that they would listen. Last month, a friend of a friend had gone to the hospital on his twenty-first to get his stomach pumped. She didn't want that to happen to Sean.

There was a knock on Sean's door.

"Yeah?"

The door swung open, and Luke stood there, looking handsome and impatient. "You ready to go yet?"

Rachel moved off Sean, so they could both sit up.

"Yeah, I'm ready," he said and got to his feet. He grabbed Rachel's hand and pulled her up next to him. "I'll see you later, okay?"

"Okay."

He kissed her neck, taking his time and working his way up to her ear. "You can give me my birthday present later," he whispered.

"Mmm...okay," she moaned in reply.

Luke cleared his throat, and Rachel jumped. She'd forgotten that he was there.

Sean chuckled and kissed her again, this time on the forehead. She'd already forbidden him from kissing her on the lips in hopes that he wouldn't get sick, too.

"I'm coming." He squeezed Rachel's hand and walked out the door, past his roommate.

Luke turned to follow, but Rachel stopped him. "Luke?"

"What?"

Rachel stepped closer. "You'd better bring Sean home tonight—alive." She tried to sound threatening, but it was hard to do with her nose stuffed and her words coming out sounding more like a three-year-old was talking than a nine-teen-year-old.

"Okay, germy," he said with a laugh.

"I'm serious."

Luke dropped his smile. "I promise, I won't let anything bad happen to him."

She lifted her chin. "Thank you."

Luke hit his hand once against the doorframe, and then he was gone.

She heard the guys in the living room, putting on their coats and heading out the door. There was some yelling back and forth outside about who was driving. Then, the car doors closed, and they drove away.

Rachel grabbed her traveling toothbrush and toothpaste from her purse and brushed her teeth. She then raided Sean's dresser until she found sweatpants and a sweatshirt. She removed her jeans and sweater and put on Sean's clothes. Despite them being only mediums, they were still big on her. But comfy.

She grabbed the box of tissues she'd brought with her and a bottled water from the fridge, and then she hunkered down in Sean's bed. Grabbing the remote, she changed channels on the TV until she found an old movie to watch. She was grateful that Sean had told her to stay. In her dorm, she either had to sit on the couch to watch television or lie in bed, doing nothing since her bed was directly over the thing. This way, she got to do both.

Not that it mattered.

Twenty minutes after settling in, she buried her nose in Sean's pillow, breathing him in.

I'll just stay like this until the commercial's over, she thought.

Thirty seconds later, it was lights out.

Sean turned off the TV, plunging his room into darkness, except for the glow of his alarm clock and the moon shining through the curtains.

He wobbled a little as he stripped off all of his clothes. He was drunk but not as much as he'd expected to be on his birthday. He'd gotten a lot of crap for leaving the bar when he did, but he'd had enough fun for the night.

Once in his boxers, he went to his bathroom and brushed his teeth. It crossed his mind that he should probably shower, but he was wasted, tired, and just wanted to get under the covers, next to Rachel.

After he turned off the bathroom light, he had to pause and let his eyes adjust. Apparently, he didn't wait long enough because he ran into his doorframe on the way back to his room.

He heard the covers on his bed move as Rachel sat up.

"Sean?"

"Yeah, it's me." He stepped toward the bed and hit his shin. "Ow! Shit, that hurt."

Rachel giggled. "Are you okay?"

He sighed as he flopped down onto the bed. "Yes."

Rachel looked down at him, and he pushed a lock of her brown hair behind her ear.

"I'm sorry I woke you."

"That's okay. I slept for a good"—she turned and looked at his alarm clock—"three to four hours. Sean, what are you doing home so early? The bars aren't closed yet."

"I wanted to see you."

Rachel didn't say anything, and he wished he could read her eyes.

"What are you thinking?"

She laughed. "How much I want to kiss you, but I can't."

He pulled on her shirt. "Then, come down here, and cuddle with me."

She settled down at his side while he lifted the comforter and got his legs underneath.

He rubbed her back and resented the sweatshirt covering her. "I wish you were naked."

"Me, too. I was planning on giving you some hot lovin' on your birthday."

Sean smiled. They had yet to have sex, but he didn't mind. They'd fooled around a lot, and Rachel let him go down on her whenever he wanted, which he fucking loved. She was responsive and sexy as hell. She wasn't embarrassed of her body or of letting him know how good he made her feel.

He kissed her forehead. "It'll happen," he reassured her. And, right now, it could wait. As much as he enjoyed being sexually intimate with her, at the moment, he was tired and—he'd probably get crap for this—he was just enjoying holding Rachel.

She lightly kissed his neck but lingered there for a moment. "Yeah, well, I can't wait to feel you inside me," she said softly.

And, just like that, he went from tired to hard. He groaned to let her know he liked the way she thought.

Her answer was a snore.

Sean chuckled and kissed her head again. Once the sexy woman in his arms was better, he was going to hold her to her word.

CHAPTER NINE

Rachel was just finishing up with her Algebra homework when her phone rang. Elise had left less than forty-five minutes ago on a date with some guy she'd met in one of her classes, and she had made Rachel promise to call her in an hour to see if she needed bailing out. That was also why Elise had picked a Wednesday night rather than a weekend. It was always easier to use the I-have-an-early-class excuse to end a night prematurely.

Rachel picked up on the second ring without bothering to check who was on the other end, figuring it was her friend. "Sick of him already?"

There was a pause and then, "Rachel?"

"Yeah?"

"It's Luke."

Rachel frowned. *That's odd. Why would he be calling me?*

"Are you busy?"

"Uh...not really."

"Can you come over here?"

"Uh..." Rachel was confused.

Sean had told her that he was working out and then meeting with a study group tonight. Plus, he wouldn't have his roommate call her. If he wanted her to come over, he'd call her himself. She had a momentary thought that Luke was hitting on her, but he wouldn't do that to Sean. Besides, Luke had never shown the slightest bit of interest in Rachel. If anything, Luke was trying to hide an attraction to Elise.

Luke sighed. "Look, about a half hour ago, Sean's mom called. After that, he went into his room, and he hasn't come out since. Not even when we offered him free pizza. And he won't talk to any of us. I think you should come over here."

"I'll be there in ten."

Rachel hung up with Luke and immediately called Elise as she grabbed her jacket and put on her shoes. Thankfully, Elise's date was going well, and she didn't need Rachel to bail her out.

"Keep me updated," she told Rachel before hanging up.

When Rachel got to Sean's, his roommates didn't say anything. Luke just shook his head, as if to say Sean hadn't come out of his room yet.

Rachel knocked on Sean's bedroom door. When Sean didn't answer, she slowly pushed it open. Sean was sitting on his bed, facing the wall. He didn't turn around.

Rachel shrugged off her coat and cautiously approached her boyfriend. He was wearing a T-shirt and nylon shorts, and his hair was stuck to his head. He looked like he'd come back from the gym but not showered yet. He played with his silver ring and stared off into space.

"Sean?" She moved closer and crouched in front of him. "Sean?"

He sluggishly turned his head, as if in a daze, and looked at her.

"Hey," she said, giving him a small smile. "Are you okay?"

He lifted his hand and brushed a finger down her cheek. He looked so sad.

Rachel grabbed his hand and clutched it in hers. "Baby, what's wrong?"

"My mom called."

"I heard."

"My uncle..." Sean swallowed. "My uncle died."

"Oh, Sean." She lifted his hand and brought it to her mouth, kissing the back of it.

Sean looked away from her to the floor. "I haven't seen him for a few years. I should've..." He trailed off as tears filled his eyes. "I should've visited him. I kept telling myself I had time."

Regret was a bitch to deal with, and her heart went out to him.

Rachel moved to sit beside him. She pulled Sean into her arms and hugged him close and tight. She guided Sean back onto the bed and held him. "It's okay to cry. I promise, I won't tell anyone."

Sean snorted a laugh, but then he buried his face in her neck and let the tears go. Rachel rubbed his back and muttered soothing words.

Rachel opened her eyes to Sean's ceiling. He was lying beside her on his stomach with his nose still buried in her neck and an arm around her waist. He shifted beside her and rolled over. She hadn't wanted to wake him, but she must have moved or made a noise.

Sean opened his eyes and smiled at her.

She rolled toward him. "Sorry I woke you."

"It's okay," he said, his voice hoarse from sleep.

She reached out and caressed his chest. "Are you okay?" She closed her eyes for a moment. "Stupid question. Of course you're not okay."

He put his hand on hers. "I'm a little better now. Especially since you're here."

His comment sent warm tingles down her body.

"I'm glad I could help."

Sean looked down at himself. "I need to shower. I'm surprised you were able to put up with my man stink."

Rachel moved closer, pushed her nose into his neck, and inhaled. "I happen to like your man stink." She wasn't lying. There was something about the way a man smelled that made her feel things all the way from contentment to desire. Particularly Sean's smell.

He tucked his chin to his chest and took her lips in a slow kiss. It heated her up on the inside, but it was different from his usual kisses. This one said, *I'm glad you're here*, more than, *I want your body.*

When he pulled away, he asked, "Keep me company in the shower?"

Rachel nodded.

It had been over a week since Sean's birthday and still no

sex. But she had a feeling that he was asking her more for comfort than for sexual reasons.

Sean led her into the bathroom, and they stripped off their clothes and got under the hot spray. Rachel watched the water slide down Sean's thin, muscular body. She lathered soap in her hands and slid them down the rigid planes of his chest and stomach, the only hair a thin line that led from his belly button to his groin. He closed his eyes and pushed his head under the stream.

She flicked her thumbs over his nipples and fingered the ring on his left side. "When did you get this?"

Sean straightened and looked down at her hand. "When I was eighteen. It was an impulsive move. Sometimes, I think about taking it out, but then I forget about it. It's such a part of me now."

Rachel shook her head. "I don't think you should get rid of it. I like it."

He smiled. "Then, I'll keep it."

She moved her fingers lower until she reached his left hip and the tattoo there. "Another impulsive move?"

He chuckled. "Yes. I got them at the same time."

"Why a devil?"

He shrugged. "Why not?"

"I don't think it's you."

"I was a senior in high school and the little brother of Dean and Brian King. I wanted everyone to think I was a badass."

She raised her brow with a grin. "Did it work?"

He laughed. "Hell no. I got a lot of crap in the locker room about it."

Sean had told Rachel that he wrestled from elementary school up through high school. He'd decided not to wrestle in college due to dislocating his shoulder. After the injury, it'd continued to pop out when he wrestled. He could have opted for surgery, but he'd told her that he was never that good anyway, so he'd chosen to quit after his senior year.

"Turn around," she told him now that she had reached his waist.

"Babe, you missed the most important part," he teased as he did as she'd requested.

She hadn't missed it. She was planning to come back to it.

She shampooed his hair and then soaped up his back and sexy-as-hell ass. It was small, like the rest of him, but it wasn't flat. He filled out the back of his jeans very nicely.

Rachel felt the familiar pull between her legs as she took care of her boyfriend, and when she spoke again, her voice came out as a croak, "Tur—" She cleared her throat. "Turn back."

When he faced her again, she looked up into his eyes, expecting to see a knowing smirk since he'd probably guessed what she was going to wash next. But there was no cocky smile, and it was another thing she liked about this guy.

She put more body wash in her hands and knelt down in front of him. She started washing his legs from the ankles up. She heard Sean groan, but he didn't say anything, and she steadily worked her way up. When she reached his semi-hard penis, she wrapped both hands around it and stroked until it became a full-fledged hard-on.

"I bet there was no teasing about this in the locker room," Rachel said.

Sean touched the top of her head in a light caress and smiled. He didn't reply, but she knew that he had to know he wasn't small. He wasn't the biggest guy in the world—at least, according to porn she'd seen—but he was not small or even average. His dick didn't match the rest of his body. The first time she'd pulled down his pants, she'd been surprised. She shouldn't have been because she'd already touched him, but seeing him in the buff was a sight.

His cock was long and thick and perfectly proportioned, in her opinion. From the base to the tip, it gradually broadened, and she ached to feel this wide head inside her. Her ex wasn't nearly as big, and there was a slight fear that Sean's would hurt. But, boy, oh boy, would it be worth it.

She gave Sean a small push, and he stepped back under the spray and washed the soap off his body. Once his body was rinsed, she pulled on his legs, and he moved back in front of her.

"Let me take care of you," she whispered.

She got up on her knees and licked the slit of his head. She tasted the water from the shower and Sean's pre-cum. She groaned as she took more of him in her mouth. She hadn't really liked giving head before Sean, but there was something about a guy who could take it or leave it that made it more appealing. Her ex had thought getting a blow job was his right as a man. She'd practically had to beg Sean to let her take him in her mouth because he'd rather be giving her pleasure than getting it.

She suspected he didn't argue with her today because he was still raw from the news of his uncle's passing. That made her more determined to make him feel good.

She took him into her mouth as far as possible and used her fist to make up for what she couldn't fit. She took her time in licking, sucking, and even kissing his dick, just like he did when he went down on her. She had one hand on his stomach, and she felt his breathing pick up as his cock started to swell. He was getting close, and his next words confirmed it.

"Rach, I'm going to come."

She pulled her mouth away to say, "Please, let me finish. Let me do this for you."

He hesitated, rubbing his hand down her cheek, and then he nodded.

Sean had never let himself finish in her mouth.

She licked the large vein from base to tip and took him in her mouth again. She pumped him in her fist and sucked. Within seconds, he exploded in her mouth, and she swallowed him down.

CHAPTER TEN

Sean toweled Rachel off, and they picked up their clothes off the floor.

Sean opened the bathroom door a crack and shouted, "Clear the hallway." He waited a few seconds and then opened it all the way before ushering her into his room.

"You guys have a code for getting out of the shower?"

He lifted a shoulder. "Only when a female is present. I couldn't care less if they saw my junk." He threw his clothes into his hamper. He removed his towel, and it followed his shirt and shorts. He stalked toward her and grabbed her clothes. "I, however"—he threw her items over his shoulder—"do not want anyone to see your junk."

She lifted her eyebrows. "I have junk, huh?"

He whipped off her towel. "Did I say junk?"

She nodded, trying not to smile.

He grabbed her ass and yanked her toward him. He cupped a breast in his hand and pulled her nipple into his mouth.

"Oh God."

He released her and looked up in thought. "What's the opposite of junk?"

"What?" She could hardly think after he sucked on her like that, and he wanted to pull out the thesaurus for antonyms.

"Stuff?" He shook his head. "No, you don't have stuff." He kissed her other nipple and looked up again. "Goods?" Another head shake. "Nah, that's not good enough. No pun intended." He met her eyes. "I know," he said, his eyes full of heat. "Possessions."

"Possessions?" she asked, a little breathless.

"Yes. You have possessions, which is perfect because I want to possess you, Rachel Garwood."

Rachel pulled Sean's head down, so she could kiss him. Words weren't enough to show him how hot he made her. As her tongue tangled with his, she took his hand from her ass and slipped it between her legs.

He groaned upon feeling her wetness.

She pulled away from his lips. "Make love to me, Sean," she whispered.

He kissed her again and steered her toward his bed. "Lie back."

She got on the bed while Sean knelt in front of her.

"Put your feet on my shoulders."

She loved it when he went down on her, but she couldn't stop the disappointment from entering her head.

He looked up at her face. "Don't worry. I'm going to fuck you. I just need to make you come with my mouth first."

Rachel, who'd been holding herself up on her elbows,

collapsed down on the bed. She might as well enjoy his fantastic mouth.

"Just give me five orgasms, and then we'll get down to business."

She jerked her head up. *"Five?"*

Sean was trying to look serious, but she could see a twinkle in his blue eyes.

"One," she negotiated.

He kissed the inside of her thigh and then sucked on the tender skin there. "Four."

She sucked in a breath but held firm. "One."

He moved to her other thigh, but this time, he went higher. "Three."

Her head dropped back to the bed, and she moaned as he circled her clit with his tongue. "Two. And that's my final offer." She pulled on his hair as he teased her with his mouth. "But you'd better make it quick. I'm only giving you ten minutes."

Sean straightened and met her eyes. "Baby, as if that's even a challenge."

Of course, he was right. It took less than six.

At least, that was what he said. Rachel was too busy coming to look at the clock.

Sean stood. "Move up on the bed."

Rachel took a couple of deep breaths and did as he'd said. She stared at Sean and realized that it didn't matter how tall he was. He was perfection. Muscles on his body, fire in his eyes, and a hard cock, all enveloped up in a Sean package.

She let her legs fall to the sides and opened her arms. "Please, don't make me wait."

He smiled as he put one knee on the bed and crawled toward her. He stopped when he was between her legs. "Are you ready for me?"

The two of them had previously discussed birth control. Since they were both clean, exclusive, and Rachel was on the pill, they had decided, when the time came, no condoms would be needed.

More than you know. "Yes."

He rubbed the head of his dick between her wet folds and then pushed inside her about an inch. He pulled out and rubbed his cock on her sensitive clit.

She shrieked but only in surprise. She looked up into his eyes.

"I just wanted to make sure you were paying attention. I want you to watch me while I take you."

She arched her hips in answer, trying to put him back inside her.

Sean swiped his penis through her wetness again and then began to drive himself inside her all the way.

She felt her vaginal wall stretch, and she could actually see his shaft press up against her lower abdomen from inside her as he strained to seat himself to the hilt.

He was big, she was small, and it had been some time since she had sex. He hit her cervix and couldn't go any further.

Rachel made a noise of dissatisfaction.

Sean cupped the back of her neck. "Hey."

She looked up at him.

"It's okay. I guarantee, we'll get more accustomed to each other's body."

"Promise?"

"Promise. Now, let me love you." He lowered his upper body until it was over hers, and he took her mouth again.

She wrapped her arms around his neck and kissed him back. She got so caught up in what their mouths and tongues were doing, she almost forgot about what was going on down below until Sean began to move again.

He pulled out, taking his time, and slowly pushed back in. There was a bit of pain when his penis stretched her, but it was bearable. Soon, they were moving together in a rhythm that had Rachel arching up to take as much of him as she could.

She grabbed his ass and pushed him toward her.

"Harder?" Sean asked in her ear.

"Yes. Please. Harder."

Sean slipped his right arm under her left leg, bringing her knee to her ear, and increased his rhythm. It gave him the perfect angle to hit her G-spot, and within seconds, she cried out as her orgasm consumed her body.

"Oh God. *Fuck.*"

Sean held her in his arms until her shaking stopped. He smoothed her hair back from her face. "Are you okay?"

"No. Yes. No."

He chuckled.

Her breathing was erratic, and it took her a few seconds to realize something. "You didn't come," she said to him.

His mouth twitched up into a smile. "Come on, Rach. You know me better than that. I came here to get my girl off."

Her eyes widened. So, he was like this, even when he wasn't going down on her.

"I think we still have two more orgasms to go."

"Why two?"

"So, I can get my five."

Rachel kissed Sean again as he withdrew and thrust.

By the time he buried himself deep and came inside her, he'd given her a total of six orgasms. Not that she was counting or anything.

Sean brushed back the hair on Rachel's face as she lay on his chest. Her brown hair was sweaty, and they both probably needed another shower. But, at the moment, he didn't care, and he doubted Rachel did either.

"Are you okay?" he asked her.

"Considering my limbs have turned to jelly? Yeah, I'm good."

Sean laughed and turned them over, so he was above her. "I wouldn't be doing my job if I didn't turn your limbs to jelly."

Despite her sweaty hair, her flushed face, and her jellied limbs, she was beautiful.

"How did I ever get so lucky to find you?" she asked him.

"Funny. I was thinking the same thing about you."

She grinned. "Oh, really?"

"Really."

Her smile dropped, and she looked very serious. "I love you, Sean."

The look on her face was one of determination and fear. As if she was afraid he would turn her away. Either because they'd had sex or because she'd said the L-word. Or perhaps both. What she didn't know was that he would never get enough of her.

"I don't date girls to fuck them, Rachel. I fuck girls I date." He kissed her lips. "I love you, too."

Her smile returned, and she pulled his mouth to hers. "Good. Because I want to do that again."

Sean adjusted, so he was between her legs. "Your wish is my command."

CHAPTER ELEVEN

The front door opened and closed.

"Rach? I'm home."

"In here," she called back from the walk-in closet where she was changing out of her work clothes.

Sean came around the corner and entered their bedroom. His blue eyes were bright with excitement, and Rachel smiled at her handsome live-in boyfriend.

The two of them had been together now for six years, and they'd been living together for over four years. They'd moved in together between Rachel's sophomore and junior year while Elise had gone to live with her college boyfriend. Sean had graduated that same year but started grad school right away, majoring in engineering, while Rachel finished up her teaching degree.

Sean strode toward her. "Have you started dinner yet?"

Whoever got home first was usually the one to start cooking.

"No. I just got home fifteen minutes ago."

He grabbed her hands. "Good. Let's go out."

He obviously had something exciting on his mind.

Rachel chuckled at his excitement. "No cooking and no dishes? I'm not going to complain."

He kissed her cheek. "Great. Let me change, so we can go."

Rachel exited the closet and went into their master bath to freshen up.

Now, at twenty-five, she'd been teaching for almost three years, and Sean was twenty-seven and an engineer, making his way up in his current company. Despite being a couple for so long, they still hadn't gotten married or even engaged. They'd talked about it. At first, they had been in college and too young, but now, Rachel was more than ready. They both had good careers and were in their mid-twenties.

She couldn't help but be hopeful that tonight was going to be the night that Sean proposed. She tried to squish that glimmer of hope to avoid being let down, but it wouldn't quite go away.

They went to one of their favorite restaurants. It wasn't fancy, but Sean knew how much she loved to come there, and her hope got a little bit stronger.

After they received their drinks and put in their food orders, Sean finally spoke, "So, you can probably tell that I'm excited."

She laughed. "I did notice that you seemed extra happy."

He took her hand that was closest to him in both of his, and Rachel's heart fluttered.

"You know I haven't moved up much at work."

Sean had found a good job right in the Twin Cities, but

he wasn't making much advancement, and she knew it bothered him. Maybe he'd finally gotten the raise he wanted. It only seemed like one more thing that would lead to an engagement, and she tried to tell her brain to shut up.

"Yes, I know."

"Do you remember me mentioning my dad's brother who lives in Chicago?"

Rachel had to think about it for a moment. "Oh, yes. He came to your parents' a couple of years ago. Is his name Don?"

Sean smiled. "Yes. Well, Uncle Don works at an up-and-coming company, and they are looking to hire engineers. I will automatically make ten thousand dollars more than I do now."

Rachel wanted to be happy, but she only felt disappointment and the beginning of dread. She tried to smile. "And this is in Chicago?"

"Yes! I'm getting a mid-level position with a guarantee to move up within a year."

Rachel slowly withdrew her hand from Sean's grasp. "Wow. That is some news. I'm very happy for you."

Sean's brows furrowed. "Babe. Happy for us. I want you to come with me."

Some of her dread left at the thought of Sean leaving her, but she didn't know if she could just move. Her family was here, her job was here, and most of her friends were here. Moving without a safety net scared her. "So...would things be the same between us if we moved?"

He looked confused. "Of course. Why would things change? I love you."

Why indeed.

Sean hadn't even considered proposing to her. She was just supposed to pack up her life and move several states away. After growing up with her mom, Rachel didn't know if she could do that. She'd always told herself that she would never drop everything for a man. Maybe, if Sean asked her to marry him, she would, but there was nothing stopping him from leaving her after they moved. She wouldn't be the first girl that happened to.

"I love you, too," she told him.

She couldn't say anything tonight. He was so eager about starting this job, and she couldn't ruin it for him. They could talk about things tomorrow.

"Rach?"

Rachel turned around from where she sat at the windowsill in their bedroom. "Yeah?"

Sean sat beside her and pushed her hair off her shoulder. "Babe, you've been distant all week. What's going on?"

After their dinner conversation about Sean's new job, Rachel hadn't yet discussed her reservations with him. That had been a week ago, and every day that she'd put it off, it only made things worse. But she knew, once she told Sean what she was thinking, things wouldn't be the same.

She turned to him as her eyes filled with tears. "I can't go with you, Sean."

He squinted. "What do you mean?"

"Chicago."

Sean backed away from her. "I don't understand."

"My life is here. My family, my friends, and my job. I'll make tenure at the end of the school year."

Sean knew all about her past, but he didn't seem to understand how much she needed stability and security.

"If I moved, I'd have to start all over. And who knows how long it would take me to find a job?"

"So, stay here, and finish out the year. You don't have to move until you have a job. We have a few months left on our apartment lease anyway. I'll wait for you."

"Will you though?"

A scowl crossed his face. "What the hell does that mean?"

She hadn't wanted to bring up proposing and marriage, yet she'd had to open her big mouth. "Never mind."

"No. Tell me what you mean."

"I'm just your girlfriend, nothing more."

"What the fuck, Rachel? We've been together for years. I love you."

"I love you, too." More than he would ever know. "But you've never wanted anything more from me."

"You mean, marriage?" he spit out.

Ugh. He made her feel like such a whiny girl.

"Or even an engagement."

The furrow in his brows lessened slightly. "Then, let's get engaged."

Rachel shook her head. "No."

"No?" Sean threw up his hands. "You are confusing the fuck out of me."

He didn't get it, and despite this conversation, she didn't want him to be upset.

She stood and took his face in her hands. "Sean, I'm not giving you an ultimatum. If you had wanted me to marry you, you would have already asked me. I never want to coerce the man I love into marrying me."

He put his forehead on hers. "Do you want me to stay? I already put my notice in at work, but maybe I can ask them if I can stay."

"No. I know how frustrated you've been there. And you haven't been able to find another job around here. You need to take this opportunity in Chicago. It's too good to pass up."

"So, what does this mean? Are we breaking up?"

She took a deep breath. That was just too much for her. "How about we try the long-distance thing? We'll see how it goes. We'll see how your new job goes. We'll just take it one day at a time."

"I don't like it, but I'll go with it for now."

She brushed her lips against his. "Thank you for understanding."

He kissed her, this time hotter and wetter. "We might be trying the long-distance thing, but right now, I'm still here, and I'm going to make love to you."

"Yes," she whispered as Sean sucked on her neck.

He removed their clothes and laid her on the bed. "I don't want you to ever forget me."

She adamantly shook her head. "I won't."

Sean thrust inside her, hard and deep. "I'm going to make sure you don't."

Less than a month later, Sean moved away. The two of them tried the long-distance thing. It was hard after going from living together to living four hundred miles apart. The more weeks that passed, the less they talked.

Six months after Sean went to Chicago, they both decided it was better for them to see other people. Rachel suspected that he had already met someone, but he didn't say.

She sometimes regretted not going with Sean, but at no point had he told her that he missed her and wanted her to be his wife. She knew in the end that she had made the right decision.

With time, Rachel also moved on and began dating. Life didn't end because she'd broken up with someone she loved. She thought of Sean often, but after a while, it became less and less. No matter what though, he would always hold a special place in her heart.

CHAPTER TWELVE

Rachel sat at her desk in her classroom, grading papers. The students had all gone home an hour ago, and the silence they'd left behind made it easy to get her work done for the next Monday.

Not that she needed to finish up anything quickly. She had all weekend to prepare for next week's classes. At twenty-nine, Rachel was done with the partying-every weekend thing, and right now, her relationship status was glaringly single. She'd broken up with her last boyfriend almost six months ago and not even gone on so much as a date since then.

She sighed as she took the papers and began to enter the grades into the computer. A part of her had always thought she'd be in a different spot in her life at this point. But, ever since Sean, she hadn't found anyone who made her feel the way he had. And, sometimes, she wondered what would've happened if she had moved to Chicago with him.

She looked up from her computer. But it was too late

now. He'd been gone for four years, and there was no going back on her decision at this point.

As she entered in the final grades, she couldn't help but stare at the spot where the last six assignments were missing on Brian Hansen's row. Each blank space was like a pinch to her heart. She should probably delete his name from her spreadsheet, but she hadn't been able to do so yet. There was something so final about the whole thing.

Brian had been a shy, smart student who didn't say much in front of the class. But, when he'd had one-on-one time, he had never been afraid to ask her questions. She'd loved his thirst for learning. She knew she shouldn't have favorites, but he was one of hers this year.

When Brian hadn't come to class a few days in a row, Rachel had begun to worry. It was normal for kids to miss school, but they usually only missed one or two days. The principal had informed her that Brian was in the hospital with meningitis. Rachel wasn't particularly religious, but she'd gone home and prayed for her student every night.

But, when she had seen the principal walk into her room a week and a half ago, she hadn't even had to say anything before Rachel's worst fear for her bright student had come true. The meningitis had taken poor sweet Brian much too soon. He'd only been ten years old.

Last weekend had been his funeral, which Rachel and many other teachers had attended. It was the saddest thing Rachel had ever experienced, and she never wanted to go to a funeral for someone so young again.

She finished entering the grades and closed her laptop. She stared at Brian's empty desk for a few minutes before she realized that she didn't want to go home. Something about losing her student had really shaken her up, and for some reason, it made her realize how lonely she was.

That was probably why she'd been thinking about Sean more than usual lately. She still remembered how he'd come home from his twenty-first birthday celebration early and held her while she was sick and gross.

What she wouldn't do to feel a lover's embrace around her again. Someone to go home to, someone to hold her while she cried her tears, and someone to make love to her and tell her it would all be okay again even if it wouldn't.

There was a knock on Rachel's classroom door, and she saw the red hair of her coworker and friend Shelly as she opened the door.

"Hey, a couple of us are going out for dinner and drinks. You want to come?"

Anything to not go home to an empty house right now. "Yes."

"Great. Can you be ready in thirty?"

"Yep. I'm ready now."

"Grab your stuff, and come keep me company while I finish up in my room."

"Sounds like a plan."

Rachel sat at the booth with Shelly on her side and two of their other coworkers, Julie and Laura, across from them. While Rachel and Shelly taught fourth grade, Julie taught second, and Laura taught third.

"How are you holding up?" Julie asked Rachel.

"Okay. You?"

Julie had taught Brian in second grade and seemed just as sad about Brian as she did.

"Same. It sure puts things into perspective. I go home every night and give my baby a tight squeeze."

"Me, too," Laura said. "Although mine isn't a baby anymore and doesn't let me hug him for long."

Julie had a new husband and a six-month-old daughter at home while Laura was a single mom to a four-year-old son. Thankfully, Laura's own mother lived with her and her son and was able to help out a lot.

"I just get to go home and hug Joe," Shelly joked. She hadn't been married to her husband, Joe, very long, and they had yet to have kids.

They all giggled.

Rachel picked up her glass. "Better than me. I go home and hug my cat." Her eyes widened. "Oh my God, I'm going to be an old cat lady someday." Rachel was half-kidding, but deep down, part of her worried it would be true.

Shelly bumped her shoulder against Rachel's. "No, you won't. But, if you're that worried, I can always set you up with my cousin." She wiggled her eyebrows.

"I'll...think about it."

Shelly's mouth dropped. "Really?"

Rachel rolled her eyes. "Why not?"

"*Yes,*" Shelly said.

Shelly had been trying to set Rachel up with her cousin for months, but every time Shelly asked, Rachel would say no. Rachel had been set up on blind dates before, and they always turned out less than okay. But, now, she figured she might as well go for it. If anything, it would get Shelly to stop asking.

The four of them ate dinner and ordered another round of drinks. As their cups got emptier, the other three women talked of going home to their families. Rachel had been having a good time, but now, she was beginning to feel lonely again. Part of it was thoughts of Brian, and part of it was the alcohol. The two together were not a good combination.

Rachel waited for about another half hour for her drinks to work their way out of her system, so she could drive home. But, as the other three started talking about their plans for the weekend, she excused herself to go to the restroom.

Their booth was in the front of the restaurant, and the restrooms were in the back. As she made her way there, Rachel decided she needed to do something to get out of the house that weekend. She could always go visit her parents, but now that they had an empty nest, they always seemed to have plans.

She was so lost in thought that she didn't quite watch where she was walking, and she tripped on the leg of a chair.

An arm reached out to catch her, and she heard a voice say, "Whoa."

She closed her eyes for a moment because it sounded so achingly familiar. She really needed to stop thinking about Sean.

She turned to thank the gentleman who had broken her fall thank you, but when she saw his face, the words got stuck in her throat.

"Rachel?"

It was Sean standing in front of her.

"Sean. Wow." She studied him. "You look great."

And he truly did. His blond hair was a little darker and styled differently than four years ago. He had a close-trimmed beard on his face, but it suited him. And his ocean-blue eyes were the same. Beautiful with a couple of more laugh lines around them. She noticed that Sean had gained a few more pounds of muscle. He was still thin, but she could see the definition of his biceps and pecs under his shirt.

But, mostly, he looked like home to her.

She hadn't realized exactly how much she missed him until that moment. Over the years, she'd tried to find him online, hoping that he would one day change his mind about social media so that she would have a chance to Facebook-stalk him. But she'd never been able to find him. She hadn't seen Sean for four years, and right now, all she wanted to do was throw herself into his arms.

"What are you doing here?" Rachel asked him.

He shrugged and smiled like he was embarrassed. "I live here."

She put her hand on her throat. "You moved back?"

He smiled again. "Guilty."

"Sean, introduce me."

Until that moment, her eyes had only been on Sean, but she now looked at his table to see that he was having dinner with someone. A woman someone. A beautiful, blonde-haired, green-eyed someone.

He was on a date.

The night couldn't get any worse.

"Teri, this is Rachel. We knew each other back in college. Rachel, this is Teri, my—"

Rachel stuck out her hand, cutting Sean off. "Hi, Teri. Nice to meet you." She didn't want to hear—couldn't hear Sean say that Teri was his girlfriend. Not when she'd been thinking about him all week.

Teri shook Rachel's hand, and as soon as she dropped it, Rachel stepped back.

"I'm sorry. I have to...go." She spun on her heel and went straight back to the booth, forgetting all about trying to make it to the restroom.

Rachel grabbed her coat and purse when she reached the booth.

"Rach?" Shelly asked.

"I'm sorry. I have to go. Something came up."

"Are you okay to drive?"

Now that Rachel felt like a cold bucket of water had been dumped on her head, she was as sober as could be. Sean hadn't even introduced her as his ex-girlfriend. She was just someone he'd known from college.

"Yep."

"Is everything okay?"

"It will be." Once she escaped from the restaurant and bawled her eyes out. "Please don't worry. I'll call you later."

Shelly bit her lip, and her eyes were full of concern. "Okay," she said reluctantly.

"Bye," Rachel said, trying to give her friends one last sincere smile before she practically ran for the door.

She broke into a sprint once outside and made it to her car in record time.

Once she closed the door, Rachel wanted to put her head on the steering wheel and cry, but she couldn't. *What if Sean and his girlfriend walk outside and see me?* No way could she handle that kind of humiliation right now.

She hadn't realized until that moment that a part of her always thought she and Sean would get back together someday. But he had moved back and hadn't even called her. He had a girlfriend.

That horrible conclusion went through her at the thought of Sean moving back to Minnesota for his girlfriend when Rachel hadn't been enough to get him to stay. The realization made her feel depressed, foolish, and humiliated. Even if no one else knew she hadn't been good enough, Rachel knew.

Rachel slammed the car into reverse and then drive. She peeled out of the restaurant and hurried home as fast as the speed limits allowed.

When she arrived home, she ended up standing in the entryway of her apartment, staring at the floor. Not knowing what else to do, she let her keys, purse, and jacket fall to the floor and walked down the hall to her room. As she made her way there, she stripped off her shoes and clothes. She could pick them up tomorrow.

She went straight to her bathroom and turned on the shower. Only after the water was warm and she stepped inside did Rachel give herself permission to let go and cry.

CHAPTER THIRTEEN

After she dried off, Rachel combed her hair and put on her most comfortable pair of pajamas. Then, she flopped down onto the couch. She picked up her remote, but nothing appealed to her. She wasn't as sad after her big cry, but now, she felt incredibly drained. She didn't have the energy to do anything that would require her brain to function at more than two percent.

She dropped the remote and was shuffling back down the hall to her room when she heard a knock at the door. Out of habit, she turned and walked to the entrance. It didn't occur to her until she was kicking her crap out of the way to open the door that she had no idea who would be knocking after eight p.m. on a Friday. Or that she didn't want any company and that she should just ignore the knock, go to bed, and bury herself under her covers.

Rachel wasn't normally a feel-sorry-for-yourself kind of person, but everyone deserved those days occasionally. And it was her day. Whoever was on the other side had better be prepared for some unfriendly company.

After she kicked her last item far enough to get the door open, Rachel finally figured out it had to be Shelly on the other side of the door. Her friend had been worried when Rachel left so abruptly, and she was too sweet to not check up on Rachel.

But, when she swung the door open, it wasn't Shelly on the other side. It was Sean.

Rachel had been crying. Sean could tell by her puffy eyes and red cheeks, and there was also the fact that he'd dated her for six years. He knew this woman despite their years apart.

"Sean? What are you doing here?"

"I came to see you."

Rachel stared at him.

"Can I come in?"

She blushed and stepped aside for him to enter. "Oh, sorry. Of course." She shut the door behind him. "Come in."

She showed him to her living room where there was a couch and a recliner, but neither of them sat.

"How did you find out where I lived?"

Sean smiled. "I called your mom."

"That was nice of her. She always did love you."

Rachel sniffled, and he did what he'd wanted to do since she opened the door. Since he saw her in the restaurant. He stalked toward her and took her in his arms.

"You've been crying." He wiped a lone tear from her cheek.

She lifted her chin. "Maybe."

"You can't lie to me, Rach. I know you."

She disentangled herself from his arms and took a step back. She crossed her arms over her chest. "Sean, why are you here?"

He took a step closer. "I told you, I came to see you."

"Why? I can't imagine your girlfriend likes you being here."

"Girlfriend?" *Who in the hell is she talking about?*

Rachel raised her brow at him like he was stupid. "Teri. Or did you forget that I just met her?"

Sean barked out a laugh, and Rachel scowled at him.

"I don't see how this is funny."

"Teri's not my girlfriend." He took another step closer.

Rachel rolled her eyes. "Fine. Your date."

Sean took another step and yanked her into his arms again. He buried his nose in her neck and inhaled. She still smelled the same, and his knees almost buckled.

"She wasn't my date either."

Rachel pushed against his chest, so he looked at her.

"She's a headhunter."

"Huh?"

Sean put his mouth where his nose had been and sucked on her skin. "Mmm." She still tasted the same, too.

She clutched the back of his head and drew in a breath.

He smiled. He still knew her sweet spots. He moved his mouth up to her ear. "She's a headhunter. She found me a job here. I was just meeting with her to sign the final paperwork."

Rachel had her eyes closed and tipped her head to the side to give him better access. "Headhunter?"

He nuzzled her. "Yes. She searched for a job for me, so I could move back here and settle some unfinished business." He slipped his hand up her pajama shirt and flicked his thumb over her nipple.

"And what unfinished business is that?" she asked, the words strained due to her desire.

"The business where I come back and marry the fuck out of you."

Rachel straightened and arched back as far as his arms would allow to meet his gaze. "What?"

"I made a mistake all those years ago. I should never have left you." He stared into her hazel eyes. "I should have asked you to marry me. I would like to say I was young and dumb, but at twenty-seven, I think I was just dumb. I have missed you every day."

"Why didn't you say something sooner?"

He shrugged. "I don't know. I felt stupid. I didn't want to be wrong. I don't know. It took me a while to comprehend that no other woman would ever be as good as you. When I did realize that, I knew I couldn't let what I'd sacrificed go to waste. I put my time in at my company, got my experience, and moved up so that, when I moved back to Minnesota, I could get a good job."

"And here you are." Her voice didn't sound like she was on board with him.

"Here I am."

"And why am I just hearing about this tonight? How do

you know I'm not already in a relationship? Do you know how crazy you sound?"

He laughed. "I wanted to surprise you after I had everything in order, but us running into each other tonight changed my plans. I know you haven't dated anyone for about six months or so."

Her mouth dropped open.

"You shouldn't post so much stuff on social media."

"But..."

"I might not have accounts, but I know people who do."

She tried to look stern, but he dismissed her expression and continued on, "And I might sound crazy, but it's only because I'm crazy in love."

"Now, you just sound cheesy."

He laughed again. "Yeah, so? It's true. I love you, Rachel Garwood. I want you to be my wife and for us to live happily ever after. I'm sorry it took me so long to understand that."

Rachel put her head in her hand. "This is crazy."

"I believe you already said that."

She peered up at him. "But it's true."

"Do you love me?" He knew he was taking a big gamble, asking her that after they'd been apart for so long.

She swallowed and closed her eyes. "Yes. I realized that tonight more than ever. I still love you."

"Fuck yeah." Sean pulled her close and kissed her.

She pushed against his chest again. "But we can't get married right away. People will think we're crazy."

He sighed. "I'm beginning to hate that word."

She laughed. "It's true."

"As long as you agree right now to marry me, I can wait as

long as you need." He thought about what he'd said. "I amend my statement. I will give you two years, and then I'm hauling you to the justice of the peace. I can only wait so long to be your husband and put my babies in you."

Rachel's hazel eyes filled with tears.

He touched his forehead to hers. "Baby, you're not supposed to cry."

"These are happy tears."

"They are?"

She nodded. "Yes. Yes, I'll marry you, but we are going to wait at least a year."

He rolled his eyes but then smiled. "Okay, I'll take it. I love you."

"I love you, too."

He'd never heard sweeter words. He kissed her and then pulled away. "Can I make love to you now, fiancée?"

She wrapped her arms around his neck. "I thought you'd never ask."

EPILOGUE

PRESENT DAY

"There you are."

Rachel looked from her husband on the dance floor to her friend and bridesmaid Elise. "Yeah, I had to give the old feet a break."

"Ah, yes, beauty before comfort." Elise tapped her chin. "Maybe I should rethink my shoe selection." Elise was going to marry Sean's old college roommate Luke next May. She wrinkled her nose. "Nah, worth it."

Rachel laughed. "That's what I thought."

She grabbed her high heels and slipped her feet inside. She got to her feet just as a set of arms clothed in a black tux went around Elise's waist.

Luke kissed Elise's neck. "What are you two talking about over here, in the corner?"

"Shoes," Rachel told Elise's fiancé.

"Boring."

Elise tipped her head back. "To you maybe, but to us ladies, it's serious business."

"If you say so," Luke said as he leaned over and kissed her. "Now that you mention serious business, I have some *serious business* to discuss with you upstairs."

Rachel and Sean's wedding reception was at a hotel so that everyone could go up to their floors after, and they wouldn't have to worry about driving drunk.

Elise rolled her eyes, but Rachel could see that Elise wanted to take Luke up on his offer. Rachel was about to tell the two of them to go when another set of arms came around her waist in an almost identical tux and pulled her back into a hard chest.

"Are you doing okay, wife?"

Rachel cuddled into Sean's chest. "Yes, husband. I was just about to tell Elise and Luke good night, so they could go hump like bunnies."

"*Rachel,*" Elise said while Sean and Luke laughed.

Rachel shrugged. "It's true."

"Speaking of humping like bunnies," Sean spoke in her ear, "do you think we can leave our own party? I have to work on putting some babies in you."

She didn't know what it was, but every time Sean talked about getting her pregnant, it turned her on like nothing else.

She spun around and wrapped her arms around his neck. "Take me upstairs, husband."

He smiled. "Yes, ma'am." He looked over her shoulder. "Sorry, guys, my wife is tired and needs to go rest."

Luke snorted, and Elise laughed with a, "Yeah, right."

Sean took Rachel's hand to lead her out the door.

Luke put out his fist. "Congratulations, man."

Sean bumped his knuckles against Luke's. "Thanks, man. Thanks for being here."

Elise gave Rachel a hug. "Congratulations, sweetie. I'm so happy for you."

Rachel felt tears prickle her eyes. "Thank you."

Elise stepped away. "You go. Luke and I will take care of your guests."

"Ah, man," Luke whined.

Rachel laughed as Sean practically ran out the door, pulling her behind him. Her feet were definitely going to hurt after this.

She looked over at her husband's golden head and the heat in his blue eyes as they entered the elevator.

Screw her feet.

Worth it.

EPILOGUE TWO

SEVERAL YEARS LATER

"**R**achel," Sean whispered from behind her in bed.

"Mm?" she replied. It was Saturday morning, and she refused to get up until she had to. She was still the queen of sleep. Unfortunately, there were many who constantly tried to take her crown. But this morning, she wasn't giving up easily.

Her husband wrapped his arm around her waist and pulled her back toward him. Her butt was immediately met with his morning erection.

"Rach, I need you."

She smiled but didn't move. "Take care of it yourself. I'm sleeping."

He flipped her onto her back and tried to scowl at her, but she could see the twinkle in his blue eyes.

Rachel burst out laughing at his expression.

Sean immediately slapped his hand over her mouth as

they both looked at their closed bedroom door. They lay there frozen, waiting, but thankfully, nothing happened.

Her husband slowly moved his hand away and kissed her.

She wrapped her arms around his neck and opened her mouth for him. She didn't know how he did it, but her husband was a better kisser than he had been in college. And he'd been phenomenal back then.

Sean slid his hand inside her pajama pants and between her legs. He lifted his head. "I need to taste you. It's been too long." He raised his eyebrow and smiled. "So, you see, I can't take care of it myself."

Rachel chuckled, threw her arms up over her head, and closed her eyes. "Okay, I'll lay here and doze while you go down on me," she joked.

Sean pushed two fingers into her and went straight for her G-spot.

Her eyes flew open.

Sean brushed his hand over her eyes to close them. "Shh...go back to sleep," he said with a grin on his face. He had to know she wasn't going to be sleeping now.

She clutched the hair at the back of his head. "I changed my mind."

"Oh...so the lady likes what the gentleman is doing, huh?"

Rachel moaned softly. "You know she does."

"God, I can't wait to go down on you."

"Only if you make love to me afterwards."

Sean kissed her and shook his head. "No can do. We have a little over a week left."

"I hate this."

"I do, too. But do you want another Allison situation?"

"You're right. No sex until you're cleared."

Sean sat up on his knees and smiled. He glided his fingers under her pants, and just as he slowly began to slip them off, there was a pounding at the door.

"Let me in," was what the voice on the other side said, it sounded like "Yet me in."

Sean dropped his chin to his chest and sighed.

Rachel patted his knee. "You might as well get the door."

Sean reluctantly got out of bed and went to the door as Rachel pulled up her pants.

Sean unlocked the knob and opened the door.

A flying mass of blonde hair and blue pajamas hurled straight for their bed. "Momma, momma," said three-year-old Jack as he climbed onto the bed. He laid down next to Rachel. "I missed you."

She kissed his forehead. "I missed you too, buddy."

Sean came over and laid down on the other side of Jack. "What about me? Did you miss Daddy?"

"Um..." He put his finger to his mouth and thought about it. "Yes."

"Thanks," Sean said dryly.

"Momma, I heard Allison crying, so I brought her in here," six-year-old Ella said, as she walked into the bedroom.

"Ella, what have Daddy and I said about getting the baby?" Rachel asked while Sean got out of bed and took one-year old Allison from her sister.

"That I should come and get you first," Ella answered.

"That's right."

"I'll remember next time."

Rachel would believe it when she saw it. Ella always said that, and then always picked up her sister from the crib. One of these days, Ella was going to drop Allison, but Ella didn't quite understand she wasn't big enough to help.

"Alright. Since everyone's up, we might as well go downstairs and make pancakes," Rachel announced.

"Yay!" Ella and Jack said.

Rachel got up from bed as the two older kids ran from their room. She walked over to Sean and took the baby. "Hey, sweat pea." Rachel kissed her on the cheek. "Daddy and I were just talking about you."

Sean laughed. "Yeah, but it was how you haven't always been sweet. No offense, baby, but we can't handle another one of you."

Allison had been a handful from the moment she was born. She'd had colic and acid reflux, and she had never slept more than two hours at a time until she was over six months old. She was the reason Sean had gotten a vasectomy a couple weeks ago. Rachel and Sean were in their late thirties now, and they'd decided they couldn't handle another baby.

As if Allison knew what her parents were saying about her, she giggled and slapped her hand on Rachel's face.

"Do you want to make pancakes or change her diaper?" Sean asked. "I vote I make pancakes."

Rachel grinned. "It's a deal." Two minutes to change a diaper versus twenty minutes for pancakes. It was a no brainer to agree to his proposal.

"I'll meet you down there." He kissed Rachel and said, "Tonight we're finishing what we started."

She grabbed onto his shirt and kissed him again. "I'm holding you to it."

They left their bedroom with Sean going to the kitchen, and Rachel going to Allison's room. "Okay, sweet pea, what do you have for momma this morning."

Allison smiled up at Rachel as she laid her on the changing table. The diaper was poop free, and only took a minute to change. Rachel was glad she'd gotten out of making pancakes.

She picked up the baby and carried her to the living room. She stopped and looked around as she stood at the end of the hallway, looking into the rest of the house. Sean was in the kitchen with Ella, showing her how to stir, and Jack was in the middle of the living room floor watching TV.

"What do you think?" Rachel whispered to Allison. "Are you all worth it?"

As Allison smiled up at her momma, Rachel thought, *Totally worth it.*

FRIENDS WITH BENEFITS
SAMPLE

CHAPTER ONE

Elise Phillips scanned the bar and grill as the door closed, leaving the June warmth behind her.

An arm toward the back of the room shot up, waving. Next, she saw her college friend's light-brown hair, and then Rachel Garwood's pixie face lit up as she beckoned her to the table.

When Elise approached, Rachel stood and squealed, her hazel eyes shining, as she held out her arms for a hug. Rachel had to step on her tippy-toes while Elise had to bend down. Elise was five-seven, but Rachel was only five-two.

"I'm so happy you're here," Rachel said. "I can't believe you get to come out with us whenever you want now."

About a month ago, Elise had moved back to the Minneapolis-St. Paul area, where she'd gone to high school and college. She'd found out her father was sick, and she wanted to be close to him just in case he didn't have much time left. Even though Rachel had also been born and raised in the Twin Cities, they hadn't met until they became room-mates at the University of Minnesota.

"Me either," she said as she stepped back from her friend.

"So, how's the house-hunt going?" Rachel asked as she took her seat.

Elise sighed as she hung her purse on the edge of the chair next to Rachel and sat next to her. "Okay. I'm so glad my old house sold; that's a relief. I really like the realtor you referred, but so far, I haven't found something I really like and want to buy."

"I'm so glad you like Cara. She's great. And I know what you mean. Sean probably would have been happy with the ten other houses we saw, but I didn't have that I-could-live-here feeling." Rachel had just bought a home with her fiancé, Sean, about six months earlier. "I'm sure you'll find one you like sooner rather than later."

"I hope so. I can only live with my parents for so long before they drive me completely nuts. I'm twenty-nine, but sometimes, I think they forget that I've been living on my own for over a decade."

"Ah, they're sweet."

Elise snorted. "You don't have to live with them."

Her mother had always been protective, but her hovering had gotten worse ever since her father was diagnosed with colon cancer.

"Well, let's agree to disagree. I'm just happy you're home."

So was she. Elise had enjoyed living in Denver since finishing graduate school, but it felt good to be home. And, while she would miss it, she didn't regret coming back once she learned her father was sick.

Elise gestured to the four open seats at the table. "Who else is coming?"

"Do you remember Shelly and Joe Howard?"

"Hmm." Elise couldn't quite remember them off the top of her head. "Oh. Did I meet them one year at your Christmas party? Shelly teaches with you, and her boyfriend is Joe. Both redheads?"

"Yes, that's them. Although they're husband and wife now. Shelly is actually pregnant. They are going to have the cutest little ginger baby."

Elise chuckled. "That's so great for them," she said, meaning it even though she felt slightly let down.

When Rachel had asked her to have dinner and drinks, Elise had assumed it was going to be a girls' thing. While she remembered liking Shelly and Joe, they were a couple, which meant one of the six seats belonged to Sean. So, either it was a couples' get-together and Rachel was setting her up with someone or she was going to be the dreaded fifth wheel. Neither option sounded appealing.

"So, Shelly, Joe, and Sean are coming. Is the sixth seat someone you're trying to hook me up with?" she asked just as Rachel said, "Oh, look. There are Shelly and Joe now."

Her friend stood and waved to catch the newcomers' attention.

Despite the two of them speaking at the same time, Rachel had heard her question. She sat back down and cocked her head. "I wouldn't do that to you. I know how much you hate being set up on blind dates."

Fifth wheel, it was then. Elise didn't know whether to be relieved that she wouldn't have to fake interest in someone— because she really didn't have the energy for that tonight—or disappointed that she was going to be the poor single girl.

Turned out neither because Rachel then said, "No, the last seat is for Luke Long. Do you remember him?"

Elise's answer was a groan of irritation. Oh, she remembered him all right. So did every other member of the student body—at least, those with ovaries. Girls' IQs dropped when Luke was around. It almost made her embarrassed to be a member of the female sex.

Thankfully, Shelly and Joe walked up, so Rachel didn't hear her response because Elise knew Sean and Luke had been good friends in college. Greetings were made, and Elise was reintroduced to the couple considering it had been a few years since she last saw them. They talked about Shelly's ever-expanding belly. She was huge, but she still had seven weeks to go. Shelly was barely over five feet while Joe was a former football player and closer to six feet tall, and they joked about how she was going to have an enormous baby. Thankfully, the group's joking had Elise almost forgetting all about the previous conversation.

When the door opened, she was sure she could feel a breeze all the way at the back of the room as Sean and Luke walked in. The two of them contrasted each other. Sean was blond and blue-eyed and only about five-eight while Luke was over six feet with thick dark brown hair and chocolate-brown eyes. Sean was showing Luke something on his phone, and Luke threw his head back and laughed, catching all the attention in the room. Elise swore she saw drool on a couple of ladies' chins.

Barf.

To be fair, Luke wasn't a horrible person, and she hadn't seen him in years, since college, so he'd probably matured... hopefully. But, back in school, he'd been quite the man-slut. While he hadn't been truly arrogant—she'd known some conceited assholes, and Luke had never been like that—he was gorgeous, and he knew it. Girls had practically thrown themselves at him, and he'd had no shame, sleeping his way through the female student body and leaving a trail of broken hearts.

Elise hadn't been a saint. She'd had a few one-night stands and even a couple of exclusive friends with benefits, but she'd like to think she'd had some discretion. She certainly hadn't slept with every guy who had hit on her.

Luke looked at one of the girls—probably ten years his junior—who was staring wide-eyed at him, and he winked at her.

Elise rolled her eyes. She might have given him too much credit on the maturing thing.

Luke and Sean reached their table, and she realized that she had watched them walk through the whole restaurant. God, she was such a hypocrite. Her only defense was that she didn't have her tongue hanging out, and she'd never been dumb enough to hop into bed with Luke.

Sean leaned down and kissed Rachel before taking the seat across from her in the middle chair. Shelly and Joe were already sitting on opposite sides of the table, so all the girls were on one side, which only left the seat directly on the other side of Elise open.

Great. This was supposed to be a relaxing night out with friends. She really didn't feel like being near King Flirt all evening.

It wasn't that she thought she was some irresistible beauty. In fact, he probably didn't even remember her. It was just that the Luke she remembered flirted with everyone who had a vagina.

Case in point, Luke walked over to Shelly and kissed her on the cheek. "Hey, gorgeous. How's my baby doing?"

Everybody laughed, even Joe. Elise snorted.

"You wish, Luke," Joe said.

Then, Luke kissed Rachel on the cheek. "Hey, beautiful. When are you going to leave that loser over there and marry me instead?"

"Never," Rachel told him with a grin on her face. "But I'll keep you in mind for when he kicks the bucket."

"Hey!" Sean exclaimed. But he was laughing, too. "I'm never dying, woman. You're stuck with me forever."

Luke went around to his side of the table and sat down across from Elise.

Sean pointed to her as Elise held out her hand to shake. "Luke, I don't know if you remember—"

"Elise Phillips," Luke said as he met her eyes. Taking her hand, he kissed the back of it, his trademark cocky smile on his face. "Of course I remember her. How could I forget?"

Like she said, flirt.

♡

Luke Long watched as Elise rolled her eyes, cupping the back of her hand where he'd kissed it, and he chuckled. He remembered that, back in college, it had always been easy to get a rise out of her, and it seemed things hadn't changed very much.

He knew she thought he was a dog, but it wasn't his fault that he liked sex and that women liked him. It wasn't as if he forced ladies to sleep with him. In fact, he usually waited for them to proposition him, and Elise probably wouldn't believe it, but he had said no a time or two.

But *she* had never been one of those girls. She'd never hit on him, and out of respect for his friendship with Sean, he'd never hit on her. Even though he knew she found him attractive. He'd seen the way she stared at him when he walked in the door today although she tried to hide it.

He always thought that one of the reasons she looked down on him so much was because there was unmistakable chemistry between them, and she hated it. While most girls had liked him back in college because he was a jock who played hockey, that hadn't seemed to impress Elise. This had only made him want to goad her more. Maybe it was the ten-year-old boy in him.

He could acknowledge that he might go a little overboard on the flirting, but flirting was fun, and he might as well drive Elise nuts since he couldn't sleep with her. Because, unlike her, he could admit he had wanted to—and apparently, still did.

She was pretty but not exceptionally beautiful, yet there was something about her. She was taller than most women, which he always liked since he was tall himself, and she was thin but not skinny. She had curves in all the right places, and she'd even filled out significantly more since college. She wasn't too big or too small. Like in Goldilocks and the Three Bears, she was *just* right. She had long dark blonde hair and large green doe-eyes. And big red lips that the guys in college had labeled DSL—dick-sucking lips.

He snickered, just thinking about it, and Elise narrowed her eyes at him.

Ha.

If she knew what he had been reminiscing about, she'd probably deck him. It was a good thing he wasn't going to tell her.

No, he wasn't going to say anything, and he'd do his best not to torture her tonight. He knew from Sean that she'd recently found out about her father's cancer, and she was busy moving and starting a new job. While Luke liked to provoke her, he'd like to think he wasn't a total asshole.

Yep, tonight was going to be nothing more than just a bunch of friends hanging out.

CHAPTER TWO

Despite Elise's initial concerns, dinner had been enjoyable, and Luke hadn't flirted much. Maybe she was right, and he had matured.

Right now, he was in a heated conversation with Sean and Joe about politics. They were all on the same side, but the conversation was still fairly animated. The women were talking about Shelly's upcoming baby shower and birth, but Elise found herself catching bits and pieces of the things Luke had to say. She was impressed with his knowledge on the subjects they were discussing. He'd obviously done his research, and she was surprised. And rather turned on.

She'd always found intelligence sexy. Not that she didn't find muscles and a hard body sexy because she was a living, breathing woman after all. It was just that she'd always been attracted to wit. But, right now, Luke was showing brains, and he already had brawn. And she was horny.

Although she'd had two beers with dinner, so that was probably the alcohol talking. That, and the fact that she hadn't been with anyone for seven months, two weeks, and four days. Not that she was counting or anything, right?

God, she missed sex.

Thankfully, she wasn't drunk, just tipsy, and she planned to keep her skirt and underwear right where they were. On her body.

But it didn't stop her from stealing glances at Luke. His deep brunette hair was short and coarse, his coffee-colored eyes were round and large, and his lips were on the full side and naturally rosy. His eyebrows were dark and thick, as were the eyelashes that she would kill for because it would mean never having to wear mascara again. His skin had a beautiful golden tan that she couldn't help but notice whenever his biceps flexed under his tight T-shirt. He was half-Caucasian and half-Asian—Chinese, if she remembered correctly—and that was where he got his dusky features from. She'd always been a sucker for brown eyes and brown hair. That described almost all of her ex-boyfriends. But none of them had been as good-looking as Luke.

Ugh.

She looked away from him and down at her beer. She should really stop drinking. Otherwise, she was going to go home, feeling sorry for herself, and end up masturbating to images of Luke going down on her while she grabbed on to his short hair.

She looked to her friends to see if they could tell what she was thinking, but they weren't even paying attention to her. She turned to look at Luke, and he was staring at her with a smirk on his face. But there was no way he could know what she had been thinking, could he?

"Okay, enough talk about babies and politics. Joe and I don't have many more kid-free nights," Shelly said, turning Elise's gaze away from Luke.

"What are you thinking, babe?" Joe asked.

"First, everyone needs to get another drink since I can't."

"Works for me," Joe said as he raised his arm to catch their waitress's attention. "I'm going to enjoy having a DD for as long as I can."

"Uh...I'm not sure I should drink anymore," Elise said.

"Why not?" Rachel asked. "Tomorrow is Saturday, and this is the first time you've come out with us since you moved back. We should be celebrating."

Elise didn't answer because she couldn't tell the whole table her lame reason for wanting to cut herself off.

"Yeah, Elise, why not?" Luke joined in.

She couldn't tell if he was mocking her or not, but she didn't want to disappoint Rachel. Elise was certain she could stop thinking about Luke sexually, so she said, "Okay, order me another beer."

"Woohoo!" Rachel said. "That's the girl I remember from college."

Elise laughed as their waitress approached.

"Refills for everyone," Sean said. "And five shots of Jägermeister," he added, wiggling his eyebrows.

Elise groaned. "Oh God. Jäger was my go-to shot in college. I used to get so drunk off that stuff."

"And that is why I ordered it."

"Your fiancé is evil," Elise told her friend.

Rachel laughed. "Nah, we just want you to have fun with some reminiscing on the side."

Their server brought back their five shots along with one shot of Coke. "I didn't want you to feel left out," she told Shelly.

"Aw, that's so sweet," Shelly said. After their waitress walked away, she added, "Someone's getting a big tip." She picked up her shot, and everyone else followed. "What are we toasting to?"

"Good friends."

"Healthy babies."

"Getting laid."

"*Sean,*" Rachel chided.

"What? I've been gone all week on business. You *know* you're going to be giving it to me later."

Rachel set her full shot glass on the table. "Yeah, but you don't have to tell everyone. I work with Shelly. I don't want her thinking you're a pervert."

Joe laughed. "Babe, you wouldn't think that about Sean, would you?"

Shelly shook her head. "Never." She put her free hand on Rachel's arm. "And, if it makes you feel any better, this baby was conceived in the back of Joe's SUV at his brother's wedding."

Everyone laughed, except for Joe, his face serious.

"Baby, we promised to never talk about that. If my mom ever finds out that I had sex in the church parking lot, she's going to make sure this baby is baptized the minute it comes out, and she'll make me attend confession every day for a year. At least."

Shelly stopped laughing. "You're right. She already thinks her Protestant daughter-in-law corrupted her Catholic son." She pointed her finger around the table. "Not a word to anyone. I can't even use the I-was-drunk-when-I-said-that, it's-not-true excuse."

Elise understood where Joe and Shelly were coming from. She hadn't grown up Catholic, but her parents were religious.

"Don't worry; we won't say anything," Rachel promised. She picked up her shot again. "Okay, where were we?"

"To good friends, healthy babies, and getting laid," Elise said.

Everyone repeated the words, and they all clinked their glasses together and downed their shots.

"Who wants to play pool? There's one table open," Sean asked after they all deposited their shot glasses on the table.

"I'm in," Joe answered.

"I'll take winner," Luke said.

The guys got up and headed toward the pool tables. Since their table was in the back of the room, the girls would have a clear view of the game without leaving their seats.

"How did Sean and Luke start hanging out again? I haven't seen him since, like, junior year or something, and I haven't heard you talk about him in forever," Elise asked.

Luke and Sean were two years older in school than Elise and Rachel. The girls had met the guys their freshman year, but Rachel hadn't started dating Sean until she was a sophomore. Sean and Luke had been roommates, and since Elise and Rachel were good friends, the four of them had seen a lot of each other. Both guys had finished their bachelor's degrees and stayed on for graduate school, but by that time, Elise had started dating Tyler. She was ashamed now by how much she'd thrown herself into that relationship. She'd barely even seen Rachel their senior year because she was so caught up with her boyfriend.

After Elise and Rachel had finished their undergraduate degrees, they'd both stayed at U of M for graduate school. Elise had been going to school full-time, working as many hours as possible, and moved in with Tyler, so she still hadn't seen Rachel that much although they both tried.

From what she remembered, the same thing had kind of happened with Luke and Sean. They had both gotten busy, seeing each other less and less, especially since Rachel and Sean lived together, until the two guys no longer hung out and then lost touch. Thankfully, that had never quite happened to Elise and Rachel, and they had remained friends, even when Elise moved to Colorado. It probably helped that Rachel was the shoulder that Elise had needed to cry on when she and Tyler broke up right before her move to Denver.

"I know. It's kind of crazy. Sean ran into Luke at our local Home Depot, of all places. Did you know that Luke works at Southdale? I was kind of surprised when I found out."

Elise knew Sean had gone to school for his MBA and worked for a big-box store. It wasn't hard to believe that Luke had graduated with a master's, too, and gotten a job at somewhere like Southdale Center, the mall in Edina. He was a womanizer, not an idiot.

She was just about to ask what Luke's role was when Rachel continued with her story, "Anyway, that's how we found out we only lived a few blocks away from him. Go figure. We'd practically been neighbors for about two years.

After that, it was almost like the two of them had never been separated."

"Good for them," Elise said. "It doesn't seem like Luke has changed all that much."

Rachel laughed. "You mean, because he's a flirt and a half? Yeah, he's still kind of a man-ho. I swear, he dates a different girl every weekend. That's probably the only thing I don't like about Sean being friends with him. But Luke has never tried to push his singleness on Sean, and Luke seems genuinely happy that the two of us are getting married."

"Joe and I have gone out with him only a few times," Shelly said. "He is totally a flirt, and the women are always eyeing him." She nodded her head toward the guys. "Like now."

Elise looked over and saw a beautiful woman sliding up to Luke and getting as close as possible to him.

"But, to give him credit," Shelly continued, "he doesn't dog on women when he comes out with us. When he spends time with us, he spends time with us. I can't even blame all the girls who hit on him. He's hot. If I were single..."

The woman hitting on him put her hand on his arm. While Luke smiled politely at her, he was standing with his feet spread apart, and his hand on his pool cue, his body facing the pool table. Elise got the distinct impression that he wasn't interested. The woman slipped a piece of paper in his back pocket and walked away. As soon as she turned, Luke took the paper out and chucked it into the trash can in the corner of the room.

Elise was impressed again because the Luke she'd known

in college probably would have ditched them all and walked out the door with the woman without a backward glance.

Luke looked up from the garbage, his eyes colliding with Elise's so swiftly that she turned back to the girls and took a couple of sips of her drink. She hoped he didn't think she'd been staring at him.

"I guess it's true that men can change," she said, almost forgetting what they had been talking about.

"Nah, we don't change that much," a deep voice said in her ear.

She jumped in her seat and turned. "Shit, you scared me." She hadn't heard Luke come up behind her.

He was way too close for her liking. He smelled wonderful, a natural muskiness with a hint of aftershave that was utterly male. She wanted to bury her nose in his neck and breathe him in.

Had she mentioned that she missed sex?

She tried not to lean too far away because she didn't want him to know that he affected her or how confused she felt when she was near him.

He tugged on a piece of her hair. "Another table opened up. Come play pool with me?"

She welcomed the distraction. Now, pool, she could definitely manage.

She raised her brow at him. "Are you sure you want to play against me?" she asked sweetly.

"Sure. You can't be that bad."

Elise just laughed.

♡

"You kicked my ass." Luke sighed, surprise showing on his face. "And here I thought, I was good with *my* stick and balls."

Elise ignored his sexual innuendo and smiled. "I asked you if you wanted to play against me," she said in a singsong voice.

Luke narrowed his eyes. "That was when I thought you were bad at pool."

She shrugged innocently. "That'll teach you to assume things about women."

He snorted. "I didn't assume you were a bad player because you were a woman."

She put one hand on her hip. "Then, why did you think I was bad?"

"Because I remember you being kind of a fuddy-duddy."

"*What?* I was not. Just because I didn't fall into bed with you like every other chick does not mean I was a fuddy-duddy." She swept her hair over her shoulder and stepped closer to him, looking him in the eye. "I'll have you know, I had plenty of sexual conquests in college. You just didn't happen to be one of them."

He grinned down at her. "See, I know you're trying to make me feel inadequate because we didn't have sex, but all you're doing is making me hard."

She rolled her eyes. "You're hopeless."

"Nah. Wanna play again?"

"Sure."

She was actually having fun with Luke. She liked playing pool, and Luke was a good opponent.

"Do you want another beer first?"

She looked into her almost-empty glass. "That'd be great." After all, she was drinking for the pregnant lady, and she'd managed to keep her hormones in check so far.

"You set up, and I'll go get us drinks."

Elise grabbed the triangle and began racking the balls, putting them in their proper place. She grabbed the one ball and put it at the apex when Rachel walked over and leaned against the side of the pool table.

"Are you having a good time?" her friend asked.

"Yeah. I'm glad you asked me to come. I totally kicked Luke's ass."

Rachel smiled, but it was hesitant.

Elise stopped what she was doing. "What's wrong?"

Rachel stood up straight. "I think we're going to take off. I don't feel well. Shelly and Joe are leaving, too. Shelly's tired, and she wants to go home and put her swollen feet up."

"Are you okay?"

"Yeah," Rachel said, putting her hand over her stomach. "I think it was something I ate."

Elise narrowed her eyes and studied her friend. "Liar. You just want to go home and get laid."

Rachel blushed. "Guilty. I haven't seen Sean for a week." She stuck her bottom lip out.

Elise laughed. "I understand. Go have fun with your man."

Rachel looked around the room, as if she was calculating the situation.

"What is it?" Elise asked.

"Nothing."

"Rachel, just spit it out. What's wrong?"

"I don't want to leave you here with Luke."

Elise shook her head. "I'll be fine. We're having fun. I'm not ready to go home yet."

Her friend looked over her shoulder to where Luke stood at the bar, talking to Sean. They seemed to be having a serious conversation. She looked back at Elise. "I just want you to be careful."

Elise tilted her head. "How do you mean?"

"It's been over six months since you and Jason broke up. I don't want to see you get hurt again."

Elise shook her head in confusion. "I still don't get it. Why would I get hurt?"

Rachel sighed. "Just don't sleep with Luke, okay? He's grown up quite a bit, but he's still Luke. I've never seen him get serious with anyone, and I don't want your heart to get broken."

Elise threw her head back and laughed. "We are just playing pool. Nothing's going to happen."

Rachel didn't laugh. "I know you haven't slept with anyone since before you and Jason broke up." She leaned in close and lowered her voice. "And I know how horny you get when you've been drinking. I also know that sex with Jason was mediocre, at best, so you're probably really jonesing for sex now. And let's face it; we both know that Luke probably fucks like a rock star."

Elise laughed again and shook her head. "Trust me, Rach, you have nothing to worry about. I am never going to sleep with Luke Long."

CHAPTER THREE

The next morning, Elise woke, flat on her stomach, disoriented, with a piercing headache that only came from a hangover. While she'd been living with her parents for about a month now, she'd often still wake up in confusion from forgetting where she was at first. It'd sometimes take her a minute to realize she wasn't in her house in Denver anymore. She opened one eye to check the time, but the alarm clock wasn't hers or the one in her parents' guest room.

She sat up, jarring her already-sore head, and let out a moan. Thankfully, dark shades were covering the windows, casting the room in shadows and hiding the evil sun.

What happened last night? Her memory was fuzzy, and it hurt to think.

She realized she was naked and pulled the sheet up to cover herself as she slowly looked around the room, recognizing nothing. Nothing but the sleeping naked male lying on the bed next to her.

Oh God. No! Panic raced through her body, and memories rose to taunt her.

She'd slept with Luke Long. She'd slept with. Luke. Long.

She whimpered and closed her eyes. She had managed to escape college without screwing the guy, only to have dirty, dirty sex with him last night. And that was only the stuff she could remember.

She was never drinking again.

If Rachel ever found out, she was going to give Elise so much shit—after she quizzed Elise on whether the whole fucks-like-a-rock-star thing was true.

Elise couldn't recall everything from last night after the rest of their friends had left the restaurant, and Luke and she had decided it would be fun to take a bunch of shots. But, now, she did know that, yes, Luke Long did indeed fuck like a rock star. Her sore vagina could attest to that.

I hate you, alcohol.

Luke shifted beside her, but the arm he had over his eyes remained where it was, and his breathing regulated and deepened again.

She really should get out of there before he woke up, but instead, she found herself staring at his beautiful body. *Why does he have to be so gorgeous?*

She moved her gaze from his face to his muscular chest and stomach and noticed a blemish of some kind. She leaned closer to look at the red mark directly above his hip.

Are those teeth marks?

A memory surfaced. She'd bitten him so hard that she

bruised him...*after* she went down on him...*again*. She dropped her head in her hand. She was such a slut.

She looked again at the wound, and her gaze moved to the thin white sheet that was covering one leg and only part of his penis. God, even flaccid, it was thick and long. She remembered thinking it was perfect. She might have even told him that she wanted to mold his dick, so she could use it on herself when she was alone. She moaned softly with embarrassment.

"Jesus, would you stop thinking? You're making my hangover ten times worse."

Elise jumped. "Would you stop scaring me?"

Luke chuckled and moved his arm from his face. His brown eyes glittered with amusement. "Sorry," he said, but his tone indicated that he wasn't the least bit remorseful.

And, now, she was regretting not getting the hell out of there right away. She looked at the floor next to the bed and only saw a few items of clothing and nothing that looked like the shirt or skirt she'd been wearing last night. Nothing to cover her up so that she could make her escape. Then, she spotted them by the door on the other side of the room and winced.

She looked at Luke, hoping maybe he'd shut his eyes in an attempt to go back to sleep, but luck was not on her side this morning, and she found him watching her. It was making her self-conscious, knowing all the naughty things she'd done with him and to him last night.

"Can you please close your eyes, so I can get dressed?"

This made Luke laugh, but she didn't find it the least bit funny. She needed to get up and out of there before Rachel called her or her parents called Rachel. She really didn't need a lecture about sleeping with Luke right now—from her parents or Rachel. Especially after she'd told her friend it was never going to happen.

"I think that ship has sailed, Lise. I already saw everything last night, babe." He looked down at her crotch. *"Everything."*

She fidgeted on the bed. First, she didn't know if she liked him shortening her name like they were close now or something, and second, she suddenly pictured him kneeling between her legs as he parted her and blew on her nether lips right before he—

Luke threw back the covers and sat up on the edge of the bed, giving her a clear view of his back. Even his back was sexy. Except for the red claw marks there.

Holy shit. Had she possessed any restraint last night?

Luke stood and walked to the door to retrieve her clothes. He didn't seem to care that he was naked because he didn't bother dressing. Of course, he had a world-class butt. Elise tried hard, but when he turned around, she couldn't help staring at his morning wood, and she grew wet between her legs.

"Can you put on some clothes, please?" Her tone was bitchier than she had meant it to be, but she really needed him to get dressed before she threw back the bedsheet and spread her legs for him, begging him to fuck her again.

He raised an eyebrow.

"I know, I know. We already had sex, so what's the big deal? And I'm sorry for being rude, but I'm finding it hard to think with you walking around..." *With your big, beautiful dick saluting me.*

Luke snickered as he tossed her clothes on the bed, as if he knew exactly what was going on in her head. But he didn't object as he went into his walk-in closet.

As soon as he was in there, she quickly yanked on her clothes, except for her underwear. She didn't see them anywhere, and since Luke would walk out at any second, she opted for going commando. It wasn't ideal since she was wearing a skirt, but at least she wasn't nude anymore.

Luke exited his closet, wearing a pair of nylon shorts and holding a T-shirt in his hand. The bite mark she'd left stood out against the light gray of his shorts. She considered just pretending like she didn't know it existed, but she was maturer than that. Or, at least, she wanted to think she was.

"I'm sorry—"

"If you apologize for fucking me..." Luke's lips were in a hard line, and his eyes had lost all humor. He almost looked hurt. "Look, we're both adults, both single, we used protection, and no one got hurt."

She sat on the side of the bed. "Well, see, that's not exactly true..." She waved her hand toward his lower body.

He shook his head, obviously not understanding. "What's not true? Are you trying to tell me you have a boyfriend?"

"No."

He frowned. "Are you saying, we didn't use protection? Because I might have been drunk, and you did almost jump the gun there the first time, but I distinctly remember using condoms."

Her cheeks got warm as she vaguely recalled pushing

him down on the sofa, slipping her underwear off, lifting her skirt, and—

"Open your eyes and watch me while I fuck you, Elise. I want you to know whose cock you're riding."

She shook her head before she turned red, clearing the memory. "No, that's not it either."

"Okay, Lise, you're just going to have to spit it out then."

"Hurt. You're hurt." She pointed to his hip and sighed. "I hurt you."

Luke lowered his head and examined her bite mark. "Oh, yeah, I remember that." He looked up at her and grinned. "I never would have taken you for a wildcat in bed, but damn, I liked it." He shrugged and put his shirt on. "Besides, I sort of got you back." He waved his hand over his neckline.

She gasped and jumped up, bolting for the bathroom. "You didn't!" she yelled at him before she flipped on the light switch. She lifted her chin up and to the side, and there it was —a big ole hickey right on her neck. Thankfully, the top she'd worn last night had a low collar, so she should be able to find a more modest shirt to cover it for work, but she sure as shit didn't know how she was going to walk into her parents' house and not let them see it.

He came up behind her. "I'd tell you I was sorry, but then I'd be lying. If it makes you feel better, I don't remember doing it, and I didn't do it on purpose."

She angled her head to look at it again. "Fat lot of good that does me. It's there whether you meant to do it or not."

He leaned in closer to her, meeting her eyes in the mirror. "Well, at least I didn't bite you," he teased.

Embarrassed, she didn't reply. Instead, she worked on

straightening her appearance. She finger-combed through her long hair to get the snarls out and used hand soap and water to get rid of the mascara that rimmed her eyes.

She almost forgot he was still there when he said, "I'm going to get coffee. I'll meet you downstairs."

She hurried up, trying to make herself look presentable, and quickly used the facilities before heading downstairs.

If she wasn't hungover and freaking out about sleeping with Luke, she would have taken the time to admire his beautiful home. But, at the moment, she wanted to forget that she had ever been there and get the hell home.

She quickly scanned the living room for her missing article of clothing, but with no luck, she met Luke in the kitchen where he handed her a glass of water and a couple of pills while the smell of coffee brewing filled the kitchen.

"Ibuprofen," he explained when she gave him a questioning look.

"Thank you," she said. Swallowing the medicine, she downed the whole glass in a few gulps. She hadn't realized how thirsty she had been until now.

She handed him the empty cup, and he put it in the sink. After he poured himself some coffee to go, he grabbed his keys off the counter.

"I rode with Sean last night, so my car's here. You need a ride, I'm assuming?"

"Yes, please."

"Do you want any coffee?"

She shook her head.

He reached for something else on the counter and handed it to her. It was her purse.

"Do you have everything?"

Everything but her underwear, but she wasn't going to tell him that. She slung her purse over her shoulder. "Yep, I'm ready."

Grab your copy of *Friends with Benefits* now!

ACKNOWLEDGMENTS

Thank you to all our fans for reading our books. You are what makes writing worth it at the end of the day!

Thank you to our beta readers for your input. You truly made our story better. We're lucky to have you and your help.

Thank you to our ARC readers and bloggers who helped spread the word. You guys are great, and we appreciate everything you do!

Thank you to our editor, Jovana Shirley, for putting in the hard work. We always value your input!

Lastly, thank you to all our family members who put up with us when we are hard at work. We are lucky to have such supportive families. We love you!

ABOUT THE AUTHOR

R.L. Kenderson is two best friends writing under one name.

Renae has always loved reading, and in third grade, she wrote her first poem where she learned she might have a knack for this writing thing. Lara remembers sneaking her grandmother's Harlequin novels when she was probably too young to be reading them, and since then, she knew she wanted to write her own.

When they met in college, they bonded over their love of reading and the TV show *Charmed*. What really spiced up their friendship was when Lara introduced Renae to romance novels. When they discovered their first vampire romance, they knew there would always be a special place in their hearts for paranormal romance. After being unable to find certain storylines and characteristics they wanted to read about in the hundreds of books they consumed, they decided to write their own.

One lives in the Minneapolis-St. Paul area and the other in the Kansas City area where they both work in the medical field during the day and a sexy author by night. They communicate through phone, email, and whole lot of messaging.

You can find them at http://www.rlkenderson.com, Facebook, Instagram, TikTok, and Goodreads. Join their reader group! Or you can email them at rlkenderson@rlkenderson .com, or sign up for their newsletter. They always love hearing from their readers.